LAKESHORE EVIL

A Lakeshore Evil Novel

Book 1

KC Harper

Cover Design by

Moonlightinked

copy. Thank you for respecting the author's work.

The Lakeshore Evil takes place in an American town. Any resemblance to actual events or locales or persons, living or dead, is entirely coincidental. *If* this was based on actual events, then the names have been changed to protect the innocent. Could this have happened? You decide.

This is more than just a tale of horror…

Prologue

1994

Lakeshore was the kind of town that was a great place to visit, but did not welcome new residents. Lakeshore was generational in the aspect that most of the families living there were descendants of the founding fathers.

Their arms were wide open to the tourists because that was their livelihood. Lakeshore had no industry, per se, that could keep it afloat financially.

A town that lived in contradiction.

They welcomed you as long as you spent your money and then moved on.

The only negative publicity the town of Lakeshore had received up to that point was when Jimmy Madison was arrested for peeping in Caroline Tilden's bedroom window the night of her prom.

Even then, the only newspaper interested in reporting it was the Lakeshore Gazette.

The Gazette was owned and operated by Caroline's mother, Eliza, needless to say, the story not only got the front page, but did so for an entire month.

Sheriff Joe Solomon had no choice but to arrest Jimmy. Eliza had threatened to focus the front page on the quality of police work in Lakeshore if he didn't. He figured a night in jail would cure Jimmy of his need to use the windows of the local girls' bedrooms as his own form of pornography.

Jimmy was released the following morning with a stern warning and some detailed memories of Caroline. He still hasn't apologized.

***

Despite the population of Lakeshore being 1,241 at that time, the town had no financial problems. Its main revenue was from tourists. Winter brought people from all around to skate and ice fish on Lake Dumont. Once frozen, the lake offered numerous activities available to suit the young and old alike.

The activities ranged from ice skating and ice fishing to ice hockey and ice broomball. The only differences between hockey and broomball were that you used a broom and a ball instead of a stick and a puck. The ball had a habit of traveling far on the ice.

Every winter Lakeshore would welcome between 500 to 600 tourists which meant the Calico, Craigmont, and Axel Tree hotels filled up faster than they could write down the names of their guests.

Lakeshore had an innovative and highly intelligent mayor in the form of Jonathan Sutton. He was the youngest mayor the town had ever elected. He was 22 when he took office in 1987.

He had proclaimed there should be at least three full streets of houses that were to remain empty at all times. The fact that Lakeshore had to turn away some tourists made him realize they needed more housing for them.

There was a new housing project that produced brand new houses for three new streets. He had the town in mind when he proclaimed they should be reserved for the winter tourist season. He made that proclamation in 1992.

That just about got Mayor Sutton run out of town, until Lakeshore experienced a dramatic increase in revenue during the first winter that followed his strange new law.

The hotels filled up with tourists quickly, which was to be expected. Any families who wanted to rent a place of their own for the winter could pick from those empty homes. The fee went up according to how many occupants there were to be per house. It was fairly easy to clean and repair the houses after their renters would leave. As time passed, more college students came to Lakeshore, which just meant a bigger security deposit and higher rent.

Despite the mayor's best efforts, he could not gain outside interest in Lakeshore during the warmer months.

He tried to push water skiing, water polo, and several different water sports to no avail. Winter was the main draw for the small town.

Mayor Sutton was never satisfied with that fact.

The town made more than enough money from rent and deposits to hire a caretaker to keep each house clean, so they would be ready for the following year.

The fact that the houses were vacant for most of the year helped considerably with the upkeep.

The rent and deposits went up each year.

There was never an empty house each winter after the first year.

Mayor Sutton was undefeated in all of his bids for re-election.

He has since run unopposed.

***

Jacob Reilly was the oldest living resident of Lakeshore in 1993. He was 86.

He was a caring man who enjoyed watching the children playing on his street. When he was too weak to walk around, he would sit on his porch.

Jacob appreciated Deirdre Hallsey. She had blonde hair, deep brown eyes, and dimples. He didn't have any unnatural attraction to the girl, he just liked her company.

The 18-year-old former high school cheerleader would bring him groceries, sit, and talk with him during warm summer evenings.

She had recently lost her grandfather and felt a bond with Jacob.

Jacob saw that she was smart and had ambition. She wanted to get into real estate. She told him she wanted to stay in Lakeshore and open up an office.

She also wanted to marry her high school sweetheart, Albert Lackledge and raise their children in her hometown.

They would talk for hours about how she thought she had a bond with apparitions or *other worldly beings,* as she explained it.

Jacob didn't go much for that subject, but he liked the company so he let her go on.

He was most impressed that she wanted to stay in Lakeshore.

Jacob owned the two story house at 2782 Sedgewood Drive. His ancestors owned it before him. In fact, his father, Alistair Reilly built that house along with many others.

He was one of the co-founders of Lakeshore.

Alistair always loved to go out after a strong rain and run his toes through the mud. He said it was the best way to commune with nature. That's why he always made it a special point to never cover the basement in any of *his* houses with cement or anything else artificial. He would jump up and down and throw a horrible fit, if anyone working with him even mentioned anything else.

He would build the rest of the house solid. His floors were stronger than anyone's, because of his extensive knowledge of lumber.

The basement having a dirt floor, also gave the occupant the option of planting a garden, provided they planted things that didn't require a lot of sunlight.

Jacob died of natural causes in December of 1993. He died without ever being married or knowing the blessings of having children.

In his will, he left most of his money to Deirdre so she could open her real estate office and get her license. She would have enough left over to buy the house in which she wanted to start her family.

Jacob loved his hometown so much, that he left his house to the town of Lakeshore in his will. The only stipulation was if they ever sold it or rented it out, the occupants would have to be a family.

A family with children.

One

May 2, 1994

Deirdre had her real estate license and her office was up and running. She had ads in all of the major newspapers around Lakeshore.

She was officially the first real estate agent of Lakeshore. All previous matters were handled by the mayor.

Deirdre made it a point to try not to sell to anyone who was not a resident. She did remember Jacob's fondness for children though.

Jonathan and Andrea Elkton had two children. 12 year old Griffin and 10 year old Katie.

The Elktons would be the first new permanent residents in Lakeshore in decades.

It was fitting that Deirdre sold them Jacob's house. What better way to celebrate his memory than to fill his house with the laughter of children.

***

When the Elktons moved into 2782 Sedgewood Drive, they appeared to be just like any other family. They fit perfectly into Lakeshore. At least that's what everyone believed.

The residents were against the idea of the Elktons moving in, until Deirdre explained to them about Jacob's wishes and that she wouldn't be where she was without his financial backing.

It was a hard sell, but she did it. The Elktons were the newest residents in Lakeshore. This could have been the shape of things to come for the small tourist town.

Unfortunately, some places were just never meant to grow.

***

Jonathan Elkton had owned a hardware store in Seattle, before he moved his family to Lakeshore. His store was located on prime real estate. It didn't take long before he was offered a large amount of money to sell out.

It took him even less time to accept the offer.

He was a tall, muscular man in his early 30s, with high cheek bones, and dark brown hair. This was an unusual combination in his family. His greatest feature, according to his wife, was his eyes. He had deep set blue eyes. Sometimes it was hard to see anything but the dark shadows under his eyebrows. This made him more intimidating when he expressed his anger.

Jonathan always believed that as head of the household, his wife and children had to obey him with no questions asked. There were consequences to any back talk or disobedience. It was the same discipline that he received as a child. He always thought his father was justified in dishing out punishment, even when young Jonathan had to stand in the corner for 8 hours straight for not covering his mouth when he coughed at the dinner table.

Jonathan wasn't shy about hitting his wife and children when he thought they deserved it. He wouldn't spank them. *He would hit them.*

His wife Andrea would try to run interference for her children so they wouldn't be hit as often.

Andrea and Jonathan met at her cousin's wedding. Jonathan was a friend of a friend. They hit it off right away.

Andrea Elkton was always small. She never grew taller than five feet. She had long brown hair and beautiful hazel eyes. Her mouth was slightly crooked when she smiled. She used to dress up and spend time to make herself look pretty. When she married Jonathan, she had to stop.

He wouldn't let her wear makeup or fix her hair. He always told her that she only did it to attract other men. She got to the point where she didn't even brush her hair anymore.

Andrea was going to leave Jonathan. Then she found out she was pregnant with Griffin.

Griffin was a mama's boy if there ever was one. He was named after Jonathan's uncle, who was the only person Jonathan respected.

Griffin always had his brown hair cut short. He had his mother's features and her hazel eyes as well.

Griffin was 6 years of age when he first tried to stop his father from hitting his mother.

He jumped between them thinking his father would stop. *He didn't.* Griffin was bruised for several weeks.

Even as a child, Griffin learned to hate his parents. He hated his father for abusing his family and he hated his mother for allowing it to happen.

When Griffin was 2 years of age, his sister Katie was born.

Katie Elkton was named after her mother's middle name and her grandmother. She shared her father's dark hair, but she had her mother's hazel eyes. Andrea said many times that Katie was the sum of the best parts of both her and Jonathan.

Katie appeared to be the only one exempt from her father's abuse. Jonathan didn't lay a hand on her until she made the same mistake that Griffin had made.

Jonathan was hitting Andrea for not fixing mashed potatoes with his meatloaf. He continually hit her in the neck and face. He always wanted the bruises to be in places that were not easily covered up, so Andrea wouldn't want to go out in public.

Jonathan was never concerned about his wife reporting him to the police.

It was only after the Elktons moved into 2782 Sedgewood Drive in Lakeshore, that Katie experienced the downside of her father's rage. Both Katie and Griffin were never allowed to play with any other children no matter where they lived.   They became each other's best friend. She called her brother Griff.

Katie would usually just run into her room and hide in her closet. She covered her ears when her abusive father directed his anger toward her mother and brother.

October 24, 1994

That night, 10 year old Katie was in her room when she heard yelling coming from downstairs. Instead of hiding in her closet as usual, she decided to leave the comfort of her room and walk onto the second floor landing. She placed her small hands on the banister rails as she looked down to the first floor.

The yelling became louder as young Katie made her way down the stairs. She had always kept herself away from the arguing.

She didn't like to see anyone hurt.

She slowly walked to the entrance of the kitchen, which is where the yelling originated. She arrived just in time to see her father punch her mother in the chest.

Katie stood there and screamed as loud as she could. Her mother was on the floor holding her hand on her chest, trying to catch her breath. Her father, still full of rage, advanced toward his daughter. The next thing Katie knew she was on the floor with blood coming out of her mouth.

What she did next surprised her parents.

She jumped back up with a smile on her face. She then proceeded to skip happily back up to her room while reciting a singsongy version of the nursery rhyme of Jack and Jill.

Griffin watched helplessly. He saw the blood on his sister's mouth as she skipped passed him. He clenched his fists in anger.

Ever since that incident, Katie would get in the middle of every argument that occurred, with the same results. She ended up creating her own nursery rhyme.

"Griff and Katie went in the closet,

to hide from a big baddy.

Mommy got hurt and so did Griff,

by a monster inside of Daddy."

December 14, 1994

Jonathan was working in the basement. He was trying to repair the furnace to no avail. He had most of his tools spread out on a blanket on the floor. He knew certain things pertaining to being a handyman, but furnace repair was out of his area of expertise.

He had Andrea hold the flashlight for him as he cursed every inanimate object in the area. He cursed the dirt floor as well.

The basement door was left open so Andrea could hear if her children needed anything. Griffin and Katie had crayons scattered all over the kitchen floor. They were coloring in their favorite books.

Jonathan kept hitting the furnace with a hammer. Andrea knew better than to say anything.

Sometimes one word was all it took.

He yelled at his wife for not holding the light steady enough. Then he made the decision that would change the Elktons forever.

"Griffin!" he yelled. "Get your ass down here and help me!"

Griffin and Katie could hear him as plain as if he was standing right over them. Griffin looked at his sister. "I don't wanna go. He's gonna hit Mom again. I don't wanna."

Katie smiled at her older brother. "Maybe it'll be different this time. Maybe the monster went away."

Griffin got angry with Katie, but not the way his father did. "How can you say that? He's always like this! I'm not going!"

Griffin got up and looked in the refrigerator.

"Griffin! Get your ass down here, now!" bellowed his father.

Katie looked concerned as Griffin made a sandwich.

"NOW!" yelled their father again. This time it startled Katie.

She got up and ran toward the basement door. "I'm coming Dadd…"

Her sentence was cut short. On her way to the basement she tripped on a turned up piece of tile and plummeted down the basement stairs.

Andrea watched in horror as she saw her little girl tumbling and rolling down the wooden stairs. Almost every time Katie's body hit a step, Andrea heard a cracking sound. By the time Katie ended up on the soft dirt floor, her body was twisted and broken. The blood oozing out of her head was already seeping into the earth.

For a brief moment, Andrea and Jonathan froze. Andrea covered her mouth as tears flowed freely. Jonathan tried to make sense of what just happened.

Griffin stood at the top of the stairs with one tear running down his cheek. He looked down at the now lifeless form of his little sister. Then he looked at his parents.

Jonathan started to breathe heavily as Andrea rushed to her daughter. He looked down at his wife. "You! You bitch! It's your fault! You killed our daughter!"

Andrea ignored him as she laid beside Katie.

***

Sheriff Artie Donovan was the first on the scene. Artie came from a long line of police officers. He was young and eager. He wanted to prove to his father, Sheriff Jackson Donovan, that he was more than qualified to be the next sheriff of Lakeshore County.

He arrived at 2782 Sedgewood Drive, by himself. He made sure he was the first one out the door. His short black hair and freckles made him Lakeshore's most eligible bachelor.

He exited his cruiser and checked his gun. The call came over as a domestic disturbance. That's all Francine could understand. She informed Artie that it sounded like a child who made the 9-1-1 call.

He looked around the outside of the house. There was nothing unusual.

After knocking several times on the front door without a response, he tried the door. *It was unlocked.*

Artie started to worry when he didn't hear any yelling. He had responded to domestic calls before. There was always yelling.

He slowly walked into the house. Not a sound could be heard. He drew his weapon and stayed close to the walls. The thoughts he entertained proved that he had one hell of an imagination. He suppressed every thought except one.

Where was everybody?

He walked slowly passed the stairwell and headed for the kitchen. As he passed the living room, he looked for signs of life. When he entered the kitchen, he saw the door to the basement open.

He slowly approached as he wondered why his backup was taking so long to arrive. He was careful to avoid the turned up corner of tile right by the open doorway as he looked downstairs.

Deputy Sheriff Artie Donovan made his way down the stairs as carefully as he could. He stopped at the last step and peered down at the lifeless body of Katie Elkton. He got on his radio and immediately called for backup, again.

He could only breathe through his mouth at that moment. There was a faint light on by the furnace. He felt his heart race as he shined his flashlight throughout the basement.

There was a young boy curled up in the fetal position in the dirt by the furnace.

Artie avoided Katie's body as he approached the boy. "Son. I'm Deputy Sheriff Artie Donovan. I'm here to help you."

Griffin sat up. "You're too late."

Artie panicked. "What...where are your parents?"

Griffin had been crying for some time. He started to cry again as he answered Artie. "They just left."

Two

April 12, 2014

Deidre Hallsey picked up her hairbrush and stood in front of her bedroom mirror as she had done every day since she could stand. At least that's how she always remembered it. If her hair wasn't perfect, then she wouldn't leave the house.

After she brushed her hair exactly 100 times, she leaned closer the mirror. Despite the fact that she had kept her figure from high school, the years were most visible in her face. She began developing Crow's Feet.

All of the long hours in the sun, and having to keep ahead of the tourists who wanted to rent a house during the busy winter season, were enough to make her wonder why she didn't have a face full of leather. The hours spent squinting on the computer didn't help either.

Her long blonde hair was as good as it would get. She grabbed the familiar blue Lakeshore Real Estate vest with her name prominently embroidered in gold on the top left pocket— CEO was in bold lettering immediately underneath her name—and walked out the door. CEO had a ring of importance to it.

Despite entering its 20th year as the sole real estate office in Lakeshore, Lakeshore Real Estate had only one other employee.

Her name was Skye Hallsey.

Skye was the only child Deirdre and Albert Lackledge had. Deirdre and Albert never married, but they lived together for a few years after Jacob died. She pushed him so hard to put a ring on her finger that she drove him clear out of Lakeshore.

In early 1998, she became pregnant with Skye. Albert assumed that was Deirdre's final attempt to corner him into marriage. He didn't even stay around long enough for Skye to be born. Deirdre gave birth to Skye on October 31, 1998. Halloween.

Deirdre always prided herself as someone who was in touch with all things supernatural. She started out by palm reading, and eventually built herself up to Medium status without ever having to prove she could indeed talk with the dead.

After the Elkton tragedy in 1994, Deirdre felt a strong connection with the house at 2782 Sedgewood Drive. Although there was never any documented proof of an actual haunting, she went on the record to say she felt supernatural disturbances in certain areas of the house; the basement, the main stairwell, and Katie Elkton's room.

In 1995, Deirdre started conducting Ghost Tours of the house. She called it the Katie Elkton Experience. Once the media got wind of what had happened, the tour was always sold out. As the years went by, interest in the tour waned. It became old news after six years. After that, it attracted only a few diehard supernatural fans who made the trek from their hometowns every year. Each year, they hoped they would actually see the ghost of Katie Elkton. There was even a website dedicated to Katie's ghost. It was called The Ghost of Lakeshore.

***

Since the house was bought and paid for by the Elktons, they still owned the property. Unfortunately, Andrea and Jonathan Elkton left Lakeshore the night their daughter fell down the basement stairs to her death, never to be seen or heard from again.

The deed sat in waiting for Griffin Elkton to claim since he was the only Elkton who wasn't dead or in hiding. The night his sister died, he was put into foster care and adopted by a couple in Duluth, Minnesota, who couldn't conceive on their own. They didn't mind that Griffin was 12 at the time. They welcomed and loved him as if he was their own.

Deirdre placed an ad in the newspaper concerning the limited time left to claim the deed. Without any response, she eventually returned the deed to the town of Lakeshore in 1995. Despite Mayor Sutton urging against her decision, she put the house back on the market. The tours continued even though, for the past several years, a total of fifteen people showed up.

Three

Skye Hallsey was a quiet child.

She grew up in a single-parent home with a mother who was away from the house more than she should have been. Having a child suffocated Deirdre. She believed if Skye's father could live without the responsibility, then she could as well.

Skye looked like a smaller version of her mother. She had long blonde hair, except Skye's hair was straight. She didn't like it styled. She had crystal blue eyes, which was unusual, because both her parents had brown eyes.

Skye became used to fending for herself. Being born on Halloween gave the other children plenty of reasons to call her witch and pumpkin face.

She liked to be called a witch.

It made her feel powerful.

As Skye got older, she decided she didn't want to be Deirdre's daughter anymore, so she no longer acknowledged her last name. She also started calling her mother by her first name.

Deirdre was so wrapped up in her own life that after Skye turned ten, she stopped using babysitters. Skye was on her own. They may have been living under the same roof, but it was as if Deirdre was not living there at all.

At the age of ten, Skye was removed from school because of all of the trouble she had gotten into. She always said the other children hated her, and that's why she had to slam Carrie Haggerty's head into the wall . . . several times.

The reports of violence toward other students continued until Lakeshore Elementary had enough. The school gave Deirdre a choice. She could remove Skye from school and have her take classes online, or Skye would suffer being expelled for an indefinite period of time.

Skye preferred online classes. It was unusual for a child of her age to take online classes in Lakeshore, but everything about Skye was unusual.

Principal Angela Bayard suspected that Skye manipulated her way into not having to go to school with her behavior. The only proof she had was the I.Q. test Skye and her classmates took, and the way Skye reacted when she found out she didn't have to physically be at school anymore.

Skye was more than pleased. She was elated.

Skye had an I.Q. of 161, which made her the smartest resident of Lakeshore . . . ever. Principal Bayard told Deirdre about how astonishing it was for Skye to be that bright. The news was overshadowed by Skye's attitude and the fact that Deirdre hadn't really listened to anything concerning her daughter.

While Deirdre was out trying to sell houses, and giving tours of the Elkton house, Skye took to the internet for more than just her classes. She became obsessed with all things supernatural after visiting a few sites. She laughed as she remembered hearing her mother bragging about her ability to sense things from the other side of the spirit world. Skye realized her lie helped to bring people to the tour.

Skye would go to the websites where people could leave messages about having their own experiences with the supernatural. She liked to go through each one and try to figure out whether they honest or just posted something to get attention. "Real, real, shit, real, shit . . ." came out of her mouth quicker than she had anticipated.

She decided to do a little research.

She assumed that if actual paranormal events occurred, then there should be something, somewhere, written about them. She wrote down every one of the events and the name of the person who wrote it. She then searched the internet for anything resembling the stories she wrote down. Sometimes it took her hours to search.

She came to the same result no matter how long it took. She was right about all of them. Well, at least the ones about which she could actually find more information.

Was there something special about her? Did she have a gift? Now she started to sound like her mother.

Skye seldom left the house. She definitely never went with her mother to work, and she'd never been to the Katie Elkton Experience tour. Skye wondered briefly if she would have a connection with Katie's ghost.

She started to change her appearance. She used her mother's darkest eye shadow around her eyes. It made her look Goth. Next, she stole some hair and nail supplies from Alan Frederick's store. She dyed her hair black. The only similarity with her previous look was that she left her hair straight. She then painted her nails black and sealed them by applying cooking oil to each nail, wiping off the excess.

She learned that online.

As Skye did more research into the paranormal, she started to believe more in the supernatural. But she wasn't quite ready to put that to the test by going into the Elkton house.

Four

The Elkton house gave Deirdre the creeps. Yet, there she was, waiting for the newest group of supernatural fans so she could take them on the tour.

Deirdre just assumed it was creepy because she already had a common bond with the undead. She waited with the anticipation of a teenage girl in line at a Justin Bieber concert for the opportunity to speak with Katie Elkton's ghost. She was also fearful of what would happen during her first communication with the dead. Would she know what to say? Would there be odd smells? Would Katie look like she did before she died, or would she be mangled and gross? Would there be any photographers there to capture the moment?

Deirdre stood at the card table with literature about the house and a lot of her business cards. The table was set up just inside the house in the entry hall. The front door was open as a welcome invitation to all of those who might want to join the tour. She ran the tour year round even though the majority of interested people came during the winter season. Deirdre didn't want to miss any potential dollars by only hosting it in the winter. People are always driving through Lakeshore.

The last winter tour netted a whopping five people. Since it was spring, she'd be lucky to get one curious visitor.

***

A familiar Lakeshore Police Department cruiser pulled into the driveway of the Elkton house. Sheriff Art Donovan got out of the car sporting a smile. He may have put on 40 pounds over the past 20 years, but he was just as agile as he was during his Deputy Sheriff days. He had a military style haircut and his trademark freckles.

He adjusted his belt as he walked toward the open door. Deirdre saw him and smiled weakly. She had hoped for someone to show up for the tour, but she wanted a paying customer. She met him on the walk.

"Good afternoon Artie," she said, trying to be pleasant.

The Sheriff let out a sigh. "Now Deirdre, you know I don't answer to that name anymore. I'm the sheriff and have been so for a decade now. I'm Art Donovan."

Deirdre scoffed at him. "That crap may work with the other residents Artie, but I'm different." She pressed her body up against his while she kissed his neck.

He gently pushed her away and grabbed her by the arm. He led her into the house as he looked around in a panic to see if anyone saw Deirdre's open display of affection. She smiled triumphantly.

Sheriff Donovan closed the front door. "What the hell? Damn it Deirdre! I can't afford for the beans to be spilled about what happened between us!"

"Oh, come on Artie," she responded. "We only fooled around a couple of times. What's the big deal?"

He rolled his eyes. "The big deal is that I was married then, and I'm still married!" He forced himself to calm down as he continued. "We had some fun during a dark time in my life, but that was then, and this is now. That has to stay buried."

"Oh, pooh! I was just trying to have a little fun," she huffed.

Sheriff Donovan opened the door. "The problem is you're always trying to have a little fun. The bad thing is you are always having fun at someone else's expense. You never stop to think of the consequences of anything you do."

Deirdre became angry at his accusations. "How dare you! You son of a bitch! You have a lot of nerve judging me! You came to me, remem…"

"Enough!" he interrupted. "I'm not doing this again with you! Especially not here! You know how I feel about this house." He looked around as if he expected something to jump out at him. He started to walk toward his car, and then spun around quickly. "I forgot why I came here in the first place." His demeanor changed instantly. The smile was back.

"Alan Frederick saw Skye stealing some things from his store. He didn't say anything at the time. He told me she didn't even try to conceal her illegal activity." He waited for her to respond to the accusations. Deirdre didn't. He continued, "Also, Mayor Sutton would like to speak to you."

She raised her brow. "So what does our wonderful leader wish to speak with me about?"

Sheriff Donovan walked back up to Deirdre. "I don't have a clue. I was in the neighborhood, he contacted me, and he asked me to stop by to deliver the message. I'm sure you'll find out when you get there."

The smile returned to Deirdre's face. "Hey Artie. Would you like to take the Katie Elkton Experience tour? I'll give you a professional discount from $20.00 to $15.00."

"No thanks," he said as he opened his car door. "Mayor's waiting."

"Who's going to be here when someone wants to take the tour?" She showed her frustration.

He shrugged his shoulder, got into his car, and drove off.

***

Mayor Jonathan Sutton's office was located in the public utilities building. When anyone would pay their electric or water bill, they would stop by the mayor's office and say hello.

Since he had been mayor for the past 27 years, he decorated his office with quite more than a few personal items. In fact, it looked more like a spare room, with coffee mugs, pictures of friends and family, and various thought-provoking posters to encourage leadership, than an actual mayor's office.

The town of Lakeshore basically informed Mayor Sutton that he could be the mayor as long as he wanted the job. So he made himself at home.

Mayor Sutton had salt and pepper highlights in his light brown hair for some years. His eyes always looked gray, but seemed to change with his mood. He had an on-again off-again Malar or Butterfly Rash on his face due to his Lupus.

He didn't mind the respect that came with being called Mayor when there was an event or occasion that warranted it, but if it was one on one, he preferred to be called Jon or Jonathan.

This was one of those times.

Deirdre stormed through his office door. She had a look of frustration mixed with a large dose of pissed off. She slammed the door shut and plopped down on the extra chair as she crossed her arms over her chest.

Mayor Sutton let out a sigh. "I can see this is going to go well, Deirdre. Good afternoon."

She glared at him. "You do realize I was waiting for my tour group at the Elkton house! We could have had . . . ."

"Two people," he interrupted. "This tour thing was a great idea for a while, but it's wasting your time and the town's. We had a good run, but it's over, Deirdre."

She stood up in frustration. "Over? We're just getting started! I have all these plans for the tour, and just last week I received three calls asking about it! Three calls Jonathan! More importantly, I am more in tune with Katie's ghost than ever before. I feel things."

"Yeah. That's kind of what I'm worried about," he said cautiously, as if he were afraid that what he had to say next would cause another World War. "We need to talk about the Elkton house."

Five

Anderson Haggler was what people would call a self-made man. He kept himself in top physical condition, with only 6% body fat. His jet black hair was taken care of every two weeks at Maurice's. His dark brown eyes worked well with his tanned body when he sought to attract the ladies. He also had several tattoos depicting Greek gods on both arms and legs.

He had a talent for cutting corners to get what he wanted. His intelligence and ability to analyze just about any situation was uncanny.

He became a millionaire at the age of 23.

First, Anderson became a wealthy woman's boy toy in order to get the tuition for law school. It was a simple matter to pick and choose from among the various women who made up the social elite. Once he showed not only his physique, but interest in being a "kept" man, all he had to do was pick the right woman.

Angelique Farlay was his target. She made her money in oil and agriculture.

Once he worked his way into her life, he played the submissive little boy. He always did what she wanted him to do, and became her arm candy with never a complaint. In return, she gave him his own bank account.

She also changed his appearance. He was dressed in only the best from Tom Ford, Vivienne Westwood, and Gucci. In later years, Anderson would have his suits tailored. His shoes were from Versace and John Lobb. He would wear only black socks, Vintage Bijan Skinny ties, and his hair would be styled by only the best that money could buy. He even had regular spa treatments and manicure sessions.

After Angelique got him into Harvard Law School using her money and influence, Anderson complained that the classes were hard and he was afraid he would fail her. She comforted him as he knew she would. She had someone on the payroll take the bar for Anderson.

Anderson Haggler then became an attorney.

He didn't care who he had to lie to or betray to get ahead. That's just how the game was played, and he played it better than anybody.

Angelique used her connections to get him into a law firm as an intern, right before she died of a heart attack. She had no history of heart problems and kept herself in remarkable shape for a woman of 63.

She left Anderson five million dollars in her will. He had the money, but now he needed experience in investing his money wisely, and in making sound business decisions. That's what he hoped to gain by working at a law firm.

He interned at Hope, Meyers, and Sheldon when he turned 26. As soon as he arrived, Anderson watched closely to see who the favorites were, and who was up for promotion. He then methodically researched the backgrounds, families, and habits of each person. His goal was to find the smallest piece of dirt on each of them so he could use it to his advantage.

He found out that Eric Jenson was cheating on his wife, so he arranged for her to be present at Eric's next rendezvous.

Craig Foster left the firm without notice. The reason was never disclosed.

Sasha Edwards was found dead in her apartment. She had apparently overdosed on Methamphetamines, which was strange because she had never even tried drugs before that incident.

The list went on.

Anderson was extremely careful with his extracurricular activities. He always found a way to plant evidence of any wrong doing on his targets.

Two birds with one stone.

He vowed he would make it to the top and in a short time, he had done just that.

With all of his competition out of the way, he slid easily into the position he wanted. He was the youngest corporate attorney in his firm's history. But even that wasn't enough. With each personal victory, his ego claimed another part of him.

Soon after he made junior partner at the age of 30, he turned his attention to a bigger target; Pamela Sheldon, one of the main partners.

Pamela was 44 at the time, and married with three beautiful children. She seemed like the perfect wife, mother, and business partner. The only thing Anderson could find on her was that she couldn't handle her liquor.

Anderson had just acquired a huge account that no one else in the firm could obtain. He told her it would be an honor if she would have one drink with him to celebrate because he respected her more than the other partners.

She stayed with him after business hours in his office to celebrate. She agreed, but only for a moment. He told her they wouldn't have anything stronger than wine since she was driving home.

He forgot to mention the Rohypnol or Roofie that he put in her drink.

Within moments, Pamela was unconscious on his office sofa. Anderson managed to get her into her own office without being noticed by the security cameras. He then took out his camera and got to work. Except he wasn't the one joining Pamela in the photo shoot.

Anderson had commissioned an underage male to enjoy the older woman. Even though she was unconscious, he posed her professionally so that no one would be the wiser.

Once the photos got to the newspaper and Pamela's family, she was finished.

By the end of the week, Anderson had made full partner. Hope and Meyers had their suspicions about Anderson's methods, but that was the main reason they made him partner.

They liked his style.

***

Anderson was 34 when he met Rachel while vacationing in Bermuda. He first saw her lying on the beach in her pink and green bikini with a Mojito in her hand. She had long black hair and dark brown eyes, just like he did.

She always had a smirk on her face as if to let people know she was ready to be bad. She had a beauty mark just to the right of the corner of her mouth, and she could have easily passed for a model with her toned and tanned body.

He could tell she had some plastic surgery done, but he approached her anyway. He stood over her and smiled. He had on a pair of ocean print swimming trunks and nothing more.

She lowered the big flower sunglasses from her brow. "I'm here with someone," she said as she silently paid respect to his physique.

"Aren't we all?" he responded without hesitating. "The real question would be whether or not we're here with the right people."

Rachel was curious about Anderson's response. She licked her lips and removed her sunglasses. "If this is your idea of foreplay, it worked," she cooed.

His smile intensified. "I don't like to play with people who don't know the rules."

She squinted at him as she tried to figure him out. "And whose rules do you usually play by?"

He crouched down beside her. "Mine. Always mine. Only mine. It's just easier when there's one set of rules. Wouldn't you agree?"

"I might," Rachel replied. "If I knew I would be rewarded for my obedience."

His eyes seemed to have peered right into her soul. "Someone would have to be completely obedient to get any reward from me."

She started to run one finger over his bare chest. "I'll follow all the rules except for one. I won't tolerate my man having sex with anyone in a room that I'm not in when it starts."

"So you have one rule for yourself?" He queried.

She nodded.

"If that's your only stipulation, then I believe we can come to an understanding. I do hate the free thinking woman," Anderson said, as a test to see if she was still interested.

"One rule for me, and the rest are yours," she replied while still smiling.

"If you would be willing to sign a pre-nup, I think we can complete this merger."

Rachel smiled and asked, "Do you have a pen?"

***

Bentley Haggler was born three months after Rachel and Anderson tied the knot. They didn't feel they needed to wait for marriage. Anderson was irate when he found out Rachel had stopped using her birth control. The last thing he wanted was an heir at that particular time.

Rachel thought it might be useful to have a child, just in case Anderson decided that having a wife was more than he bargained for. When Bentley was born, Rachel saw the little miracle she created, and her motherly instincts kicked in.

Bentley was born one month premature. He weighed only 4 pounds 6 ounces. The hospital had to make sure he was at least 5 pounds and healthy before Anderson and Rachel could take him home.

As he aged, it became apparent Bentley had light brown hair, which was in contrast to his parents' darker hair. He did have their dark brown eyes though. Anderson would always say Bentley's ears resembled his car doors being open all of the time. They protruded outward even more as he grew up.

When Anderson was out in public with Rachel and his son, he was the epitome of what a father should be. He showered Bentley with kisses and always insisted that he hold him.

Once he and his wife were alone, he didn't even acknowledge that he had a son. Rachel had to take care of Bentley, which was alright with her. Even though she tried to get Anderson more involved with his son, she understood one important fact.

Anderson neglecting his child was not the one rule she had, so he wasn't breaking their contract by being a bad father.

Bentley was diagnosed with severe asthma at an early age. He was also allergic to many things, which was a side effect of having a depressed immune system.

Rachel protected and loved her son. It was the only thing she had done right. She kept him with her when she could. She also created a perfect world in his room so he wouldn't have to go outside, ever. She even hired a tutor to home school him.

Bentley loved both his parents. Even when Anderson ignored him, he would draw happy pictures of his mother and father. He always tried to find a reason to smile.

Bentley and Katie were similar. They both responded to negativity with a smile and hope.

Rachel had lived up to her part of the deal she made with Anderson by being everything he wanted. Things went well, until March 13, 2014.

He was no longer a corporate attorney working for someone else. He was now the owner of Haggler Industries and would buy larger companies, separate them into smaller ones, and sell them off separately, earning him billions.

Rachel wanted to surprise her husband at work. She showed up early to bring him some of their cook's Crème Brule because that was his favorite. She didn't have keys to his office, but she would usually knock.

This time, the door was open.

Rachel silently walked into the office expecting to find that her husband had been murdered or kidnapped. He had made a lot of enemies getting to where he was, and that was not outside the realm of possibilities.

Instead, she heard moans coming from his lounge. She pushed the door further open and dropped the Crème Brule. She saw Anderson screwing his secretary on the sofa.

He looked up without stopping or showing surprise. "I'm almost done with her. You want next?"

She ran out of his office without saying a word, and with tears in her eyes.

***

It took him weeks to track her down. She had taken Bentley to the cabin they owned in the mountains about 45 miles from Lakeshore. They had passed through Lakeshore a few times and decided to stop during their busy winter season. They loved it so much they bought a cabin nearby.

By the time he arrived at the cabin, Rachel was at her wits end and completely distraught. Anderson remembered her only stipulation and realized he needed to mend some fences, so he called his company and let them know he would be out of reach for a month or two.

He had contingency plans for such an occasion.

Rachel had actually moved all of her and Bentley's possessions to the cabin. She didn't take any of her large pieces of furniture. She just took necessities and some odds and ends. She brought everything of Bentley's though.

Rachel couldn't understand why he all of a sudden showed real emotion. She had hoped this would be what her family needed to heal.

Six

"What am I doing wrong this time, Jonathan?!" Deirdre screamed.

Mayor Sutton's frustration was unnoticed by the yelling real estate agent. He spent almost 30 years perfecting his ability to mask his emotions. Especially around hysterical residents.

"Deirdre," he said, as calmly as he could. "You are an intelligent and somewhat well-adjusted young woman with a daughter who has yet to show her potential."

She calmed down just enough to hear what other compliments the mayor might have inside of him waiting to get out. Her look gave him permission to continue.

He sighed because all of his buttering up might be undone with what he had to say next. "I firmly believe you should put your talents to use with other projects," he said reluctantly.

With her arms folded over her chest, she glared at the mayor. "So, you want me to stop the tours? Is that why you had Artie come to my house?"

"He actually went to the Elkton house," he corrected.

"Well, I spend enough time there. It might as well be mine," Deirdre responded, with more than a hint of sarcasm.

Mayor Sutton knew that if he kept dancing around the subject, she would cut him off at every turn by claiming ignorance.

He made eye contact and dropped the smile. "The tours haven't made money in years. Heck in decades! My goal is to make Lakeshore my priority. I would expect every resident to think along the same path, but I know better. In this case though, I can pull the plug."

"I knew it! Is this because you're jealous of my gift, Jonathan?" She rebutted with a fury.

"Gift, Deirdre?" He knew he would be sorry for asking that question.

She glared right back at him. "My ability to communicate with the dead!"

Mayor Sutton lowered his head in frustration. "Oh no. Not that again."

Deirdre preached as if she were about to get her own television show. "You know the power dwells within me, Jonathan! I am kin to all that is dead!"

That was enough for Mayor Jonathan Sutton. He had played the peacekeeper for more years than he could count. He watched most of the residents grow up from adolescents into productive members of society.

Somewhere along the way, Deirdre digressed.

"That's more than enough out of you Deirdre!" He fumed. "The tours are no more as of this minute! You can't keep wasting the town's money and resources chasing ghosts! End of story, Deirdre. Now go get your table and whatever else you have at the Elkton house."

Mayor Sutton expected a ball of fire to be on its way to him after he went off on Deirdre like that, but she was abnormally calm.

That terrified him.

"You don't believe in ghosts. Do you, Jonathan?" She asked, without giving him a chance to respond. "You have to believe in ghosts, Jonathan. If you don't, it pisses them off."

Mayor Sutton was at a loss for words. There wasn't anything he could have possibly thought of to reply with to Deirdre. As far as he was concerned, their conversation was over.

"Have a great day, Deirdre," was all he could think of. "Please give my regards to any ghosts you run across while clearing out your stuff from the Elkton house. We don't want any mad spirits flying around."

He couldn't help it.

Deirdre always had to have the last word. "One last thing, Jonathan. Is there another reason you want the Elkton house vacated?"

He opened the door for her. "Now that you mention it, there's been interest in the Elkton house."

She tried to contain her surprise. "Now Jonathan, you know the house has been off the market since . . . ."

"You never took it off the market, Deirdre," he interrupted. "When you were looking for Griffin Elkton, you put the house back on the market and never took it off."

Deirdre mentally traced her steps with the house, trying to remember whether she did or didn't take it off the market.

"Well . . . even if I didn't take it off the market . . ." she replied, nervously, " . . . you know how the residents feel about having new people coming in."

"I never said anyone from out of town was interested," he said, with an accusatory tone. "I know you knew about the interested party. It's hard to keep anything a secret in Lakeshore."

"I'm glad it's all in the open," Deirdre replied, as if she was just let in on some huge secret. "So how does the rest of Lakeshore feel about adding a new resident or residents?"

"I guess you don't read the Lakeshore Gazette, Deirdre. We had a poll question in there for the past week, asking our residents if they were ready to accept outsiders into our community. Eighty eight percent of Lakeshore said we should welcome any newcomers."

Deirdre took defeat more gracefully than she did when she was victorious. There were only a few more questions.

Deirdre shot out her questions in rapid fire succession. "Who is this person? Are they bringing a family? Who gets the commission? Do they believe in ghosts? Have they seen the house yet? Will they need a tour? Do they know the history? Who gets the commission?"

Mayor Sutton's head swam with Deirdre's verbal assault. "I believe you asked the commission question twice," he responded.

She just raised a brow as if to point out the importance of that question.

"Okay. I'm going to try to answer you in the same order you asked." He took a deep breath. "It's a woman and her husband. They have one child. You get the commission. I don't know what their beliefs are concerning things not of this world. They have seen only the outside, which gives you an incredible opportunity to give them a tour of a house they already purchased. I informed them about Katie, but you can give more details when you give the tour. I already answered the commission question. In fact . . . ."

He pulled open a desk drawer and took out an envelope. He handed it to Deirdre. "That's your commission. I take it I won't be hearing anymore belly-aching about this part of the sale."

Deirdre opened the envelope and pulled out a check. Her eyes widened at the same time as the corners of her mouth formed into a smile. "Is this what they paid for the house?"

Mayor Sutton sat in his office chair and leaned back. "That's your commission."

"You're crazy!" she screamed. "Are we robbing people now just to get them to move here?"

He laughed. "I know, I know. It's ludicrous that anyone would pay four times the asking price for anything, but there it is in black and white."

"What about the paperwork?" She queried. "I didn't sign anything."

He pulled out a stack of papers from his drawer and plopped them on his desk. "Full price was paid without your signature. She wanted the house that bad. Well, any house actually, but that was the only one for sale. The buyer also signed an affidavit stating you were not present at the time of the sale, but she bought the house anyway."

Deirdre laughed nervously. She thought there was a catch. "This check is written out for almost the original asking price of the Elkton house! Is this for real?"

"Yes," the mayor replied. "You can find out all about the new owner soon."

Deirdre had a questioned look on her face. "Why? What happens soon?"

"You're going to meet the new owners tomorrow at 9am at the Elkton house. Actually, we should probably stop calling it that."

She leaned in close to the mayor. "What should we call it now?"

He reached under his desk, opened a mini fridge, and took out a diet cola. "We're going to have to start calling it the Haggler house."

Seven

April 13, 2014 8:38am.

The sky was clear, and the temperature was a cool65 degrees. It was comfortable enough to go outside without a jacket. With weather like that in April, it meant summer would be blistering.

Deirdre was already waiting by the front door. She was dressed in her black skirt and silk flowered blouse. That combination never failed when she wanted to impress her clients. She knew nothing about Mr. and Mrs. Anderson Haggler, except that they had one child.

Bentley.

Deirdre kept checking her watch. It was 8:47am. She started to tap her left heel on the cement sidewalk. She took one last look at the house and couldn't help but wonder if the new owners would make a good fit for Lakeshore.

8:52am.

She pulled the house key off of her keychain and put it on the new keychain she just bought. It was a Lakeshore keychain. She then put the copy on another keychain for Mr. Haggler.

Deirdre made sure to do her homework on Anderson Haggler. Once she found out he was worth $2.3 billion, she made sure she'd mention several other individuals involved in the real estate business, like the insurance agent, two interior decorators, the landscaper, and so on and so forth.

She was going to make sure she would earn more than just her commission. She considered retiring from real estate and becoming a concierge of sorts for the Haggler house.

Deirdre heard the sound of a truck engine at 8:59am. She looked up and saw a brand new Cadillac Escalade pull into the driveway. It was followed by a semi-truck with the words Haggler Industries on each side. The bottoms of the capital 'H' and capital 'I' hooked off to the left to resemble a check mark.

The driver's side door opened. Deirdre expected to see Anderson himself, so she unbuttoned a few buttons on her blouse, and ran her left hand through her hair to give it the wild look. She heard he liked the ladies.

Her mouth dropped when she saw that the first leg out of the Escalade belonged to a woman.

Maybe he was on the passenger's side.

Deirdre also had a variety of candy in anticipation of Bentley Haggler.

Rachel Haggler exited the vehicle, grabbed her Prada bag, and then closed the door. The familiar beep-beep of the security system told Deirdre everything she needed to know.

Mrs. Haggler was by herself.

Deirdre started to button up her blouse as Rachel Haggler approached her. Rachel had her hair down and was dressed in a short lavender Chiffon dress with a matching belt. She was wearing a pair of Giuseppe Zanotti ankle wrap T-strap high heel tan colored sandals. It was obvious she was used to the strain those particular high heels presented on her feet because she walked in them as if she were walking with the comfort of bare feet.

Rachel came up to Deirdre and smiled as she saw the real estate agent button the last button on her blouse.

"You should leave it unbuttoned for Anderson," Rachel said, sarcastically. "I'm sure he would love a peek when he gets here."

Deirdre didn't know how to respond as she presented both keys to the new owner. "I am proud to present to you and your husband . . . ."

"Please don't give me that scripted crap," Rachel interrupted. "I want to hear it in your own words."

Deirdre wasn't sure what her own words would be. She had been doing the presentations with her prepared script for so many years that she was caught off guard. All she could do was drop her mouth with a blank expression on her face.

Rachel sighed and looked at the front door of her new house. "Well, you think about that for a while. In the meantime, could you show me my house? My husband will be arriving later tonight with our son, so it's my job to prepare everything. Lucky me."

Rachel grabbed both keys from Deirdre. Before Deirdre could say anything, Rachel inserted one of the keys into the front door lock. She tried to turn the key, but without any success.

Rachel looked at Deirdre impatiently. "Seriously? What's going on? April Fools was a couple weeks ago, and to be honest, I'm not a fan of practical jokes."

Deirdre was just as surprised as the new owner. Rachel saw that in her face.

Deirdre asked, "Do you mind if I try? I can assure you no one is playing any joke on you. If they are, they got me too."

The frustrated real estate agent tried not to think about how the first meeting with the new owner was blowing up in her face. All she wanted to do was open a door she spent the last twenty years opening with ease.

Rachel's patience was at its end. She pushed Deirdre out of the way and reached for the key still in the lock. As her fingers touched it, sparks shot out. She ignored them and turned the key once more.

The key turned that time.

She tugged at the knob, but the door seemed to be stuck. Rachel flashed an angry look at Deirdre as she pulled harder.

The door finally swung open accompanied by a loud popping sound. A gush of wind originating from inside the house exited through the front door as it blasted pass Rachel and Deirdre, almost knocking them both to the ground.

In a heartbeat, all was calm, leaving two confused women staring into the house.

"What in the living hell was that?" Rachel bellowed.

Deirdre squinted as she peered into the house, as if that would enable her to see the origin of the gust of wind. She thought for a brief moment and then smiled. She started to walk into the house. "Welcome to your new house Mrs. Haggler. I think we may have company."

***

Rachel Haggler and Deirdre Hallsey stood in the entry way to the house. Rachel left the front door open to avoid any more incidents. She saw the inside of the house for the first time. It didn't impress her as much as their spacious multi-room mansion that she was used to, but there was something about that house. Any furniture and personal items that were left in the house decades ago were sold. All of the proceeds went to the town of Lakeshore.

Directly in front of, and about twenty feet away from, the two women was the stairway that led to the second floor landing. The railing was made from ornate iron and followed the contour of the stairway. It even spread out from the top of the stairs to act as a guard rail for the entire upper level. There was a walkway that branched out from the second floor landing to each room. If you were on the upper level standing on the walkway, you could look down and see who was coming in the front door. Rachel looked up through the cutaway to the second floor ceiling where she saw an ornate chandelier.

Immediately to their left was an open door which led to the den. It had been used more as a family room. The fireplace was in the corner flush against the front corner of the house. Next to the den were two bedrooms that could be used as staff quarters.

To their right was the open door to the spacious living room.

Deirdre cleared her throat and attempted to sell the new owner on some of the extra features. "The electricity has been on due to the tour schedule, but the bill has been transferred to your name. All of the other services have been turned on, including the internet, gas and water, and all satellite services you requested. Garbage pick-up is already in progress due to . . . ."

". . . The tour," Rachel interrupted.

"Why yes," Deirdre replied, uncomfortably. "I would like to mention we do offer a variety of additional services to assist you in your day-to-day activities. For a modest fee for each service . . . ."

"Cut to the chase, Ms. Hallsey," Rachel interrupted again. "It is Ms. Hallsey. Isn't it?"

Deirdre could hear the frustration in Rachel's tone. She feared the next topic would be her being a single mom. "Why yes it is," Deirdre said, matter-of-factly. Do you need help in the kitchen?"

"No," Rachel replied.

"Perhaps a cleaning service, gardener, or handy man?" Deirdre insisted.

"No, No, and . . . what was the last one?" Rachel replied, with a detectable note of irritation in her voice.

"Handy man? Well, Mrs. Haggler, I can guarantee that anyone you hire through my real estate agency will perform beyond your expectations."

"So you run a temp agency too? Why don't you show me the rest of the house?" Rachel snapped.

"This way please," Deirdre responded, as she led Rachel to the right on the first floor to a small hallway behind the living room. Before the hallway and under the stairs was another bedroom. The hallway led to the kitchen on the left. If followed straight out, it led to an outside door to the side of the house.

Deirdre led Rachel down the small hallway to the kitchen. Her eyes burned with a hidden knowledge of something that was perhaps sinister. She could not contain her excitement as she stepped into the kitchen. "Are you ready for this?" Deirdre said, with an almost maniacal determination to scare the shit out of the new owner.

Rachel seemed unimpressed by the show. "Show me what you need to show me without the drama."

Deirdre walked toward the far wall of the kitchen. There was a white door with scratch marks and pieces of the paint peeling off. In crayon at the bottom of the door was a name, a name Deirdre made sure to protect from cleaning for the sake of her tour.

Katie.

Again, Rachel was unimpressed. She shrugged her shoulders and widened her eyes as if to ask Deirdre what that had to do with her.

Deirdre looked frustrated as she grabbed the door to the basement. The door was already ajar as she pulled. Her confused look intrigued Rachel. Deirdre opened the door all the way and stood at the edge of the threshold.

Rachel walked up behind her and peered over her shoulder into the basement.

The light from the kitchen shined about halfway down the basement stairs. The bottom stairs and the entire basement itself were hidden by darkness. Both women's imaginations were unshielded by memories of every horror movie they had ever seen.

Deirdre hoped that would be the time she could communicate with the spirit of Katie Elkton. But she held onto that thought and focused her attention on a noise she swore was coming from the darkness. Like something being dragged.

She would have thought it was just wishful thinking if she hadn't seen Rachel's expression. Rachel's breathing became heavier as her eyes widened. Her mouth was open as if she was trying to say something. Rachel heard the noise!

Perhaps that moment was the one where Katie would finally show herself. Perhaps Deirdre had finally connected with her spirit after all this time.

Both women could not turn away as the dragging sound got closer to the bottom of the stairs. Rachel clutched Deirdre's arms for some kind of protection. The real estate agent smiled with confidence as she leaned slightly toward the basement.

"Katie Elkton," Deirdre said with nervous conviction. "It's okay sweetheart. No one means you any harm. We're your friends. Welcome home."

Rachel turned to Deirdre. "What kind of piece of shit did you sell me?"

Deirdre kept her attention on what was going on in the basement. "Katie? I've been waiting a long time for this. The woman behind me owns this house now. She's a wonderful woman. She has a husband, and a son about your age. Someone to play with . . . ."

"That's enough Ms. Hallsey!" Rachel interrupted. "I will not be a part of this sideshow! Mayor Sutton warned me about your crazy paranormal rantings! I will have nothing of the kind in my home!"

A creak is heard.

A creak, as if someone had just stepped on an old piece of wood used for a bottom stair. Another creak is heard as Rachel backs away from the basement door. Deirdre stayed glued to her spot with anticipation.

She hears another creak as she tries to imagine someone walking slowly up the stairs. It could be someone who had practically every bone in their body broken.

Rachel backed away slowly toward the kitchen wall as a large shadow appeared on the wall behind her.

Deirdre held her breath as the creaking became louder. She closed her eyes and tried to anticipate which manifestation of Katie she would see. Would it be the sweet little Katie before she had her accident or . . . .

She sees what appears to be a foot being placed on the first visible step.

Rachel stopped before she ran into the wall. A hand reached out and grabbed her shoulder.

"Ahhhhhhhhh!!" Rachel screamed. Deirdre screamed as if she were privy to what had just happened to the new owner, and joined her in chorus. Rachel turned and balled up her fist, ready to attack the intruder. As she swung, her fist was caught in midair and gently moved back to her side. The man who caught her fist smiled. Rachel looked confused and breathed a sigh of relief.

Her husband had arrived.

***

"It's a good thing you paid attention to those self-defense classes," Anderson Haggler said, as he showed a touch of concern.

"I thought you were supposed to arrive tonight," Rachel answered. She was more worried about the fright she had just experienced than having her husband home. "Where's Bentley?"

"Bentley found himself a nice room on the second floor." Anderson said, as he glanced over at Deirdre and smiled.

Deirdre waved nervously to Anderson. "You don't remember which room he chose, do you? By the way, it is a pleasure to make your acquaintance Mr. Haggler."

Rachel lowered her head in frustration. She had a feeling Deirdre was going to go ghost hunter on her husband.

"He chose the one all the way on the other end of the house, opposite the master bedroom," Anderson said, as he embraced his wife.

"The one that faces the front of the house? In the corner?" Deirdre interrogated.

Anderson nodded.

"That's Katie Elkton's room." The male voice came from directly behind Deirdre.

She turned quickly, and was about to scream, when she recognized the man. "Jason Kellogg! Damn it! You almost scared me to death!" She noticed he was standing in the doorway to the basement. "Were you just in the basement?"

"Yep," he replied. Jason was a tall man of about six feet. He looked like he was in his early to mid-30s. He had on the kind of work overalls an electrician might wear in the field. His face was covered in a thick beard and mustache, which were the same color as his uncombed hair. Light brown. He talked in a soft husky tone, and his fingernails were covered in something black and sticky. He had on brown steel-toe boots that looked like they were about to fall right off of his feet. He constantly pushed his hair away from his eyes as he spoke. "I was just down there cleaning the furnace to make sure the new owners had heat."

He eyed Rachel up and down. He tried to hold in his smile.

"Mayor Sutton said it might be a good thing I take care of this house," Jason continued.

Rachel glared at Jason. "Why were you working in the dark? I didn't see any lights on down there."

Jason reached over to the side of the wall by the basement door. There was a light switch. He turned it on and off with no response. Then he raised his flashlight and smiled. "Jacob Reilly designed this house without an adequate basement lighting system. I put in the switch. Now I just have to make it work."

Deirdre stepped next to the Hagglers. "Jason is a wonderful handy man." She raised an eyebrow as she looked at Rachel. "He keeps three full streets of houses clean and functional for our winter season. He's really amazing and comes highly recommended. Didn't you say you needed a handy man Mrs. Haggler?"

Rachel looked up at her husband and nodded. Anderson smiled. "Then welcome aboard Jason. You can work out the details with my wife. I'm afraid I won't be able to stay tonight. I have to make sure the cabin has been sealed up tight. I'll be here in time for breakfast though. It's been a pleasure."

Anderson kissed his wife who reluctantly let him. Jason made a mental note.

***

Rachel navigated her way through the movers. She had enough of Deirdre who stayed in the kitchen and talked with Jason.

Every once in a while someone would stop Rachel and ask her what room the treadmill went in, or whose bedroom was where. She directed all of the business furniture and workout machines to the office on the second floor, diagonally across from Bentley's room. She knew she would spend a great deal of time in there and wanted to be close to her son.

She made her way up the stairs and passed the business office on the right. She paused to admire the craftsmanship of the railing on the stairway and in the subtle designs that were added to the door frames.

Rachel stood by the first room that would also have been a good one for Bentley. The one he chose was at the far corner of the house. The bedroom door was open, and Rachel stood in the doorway as she looked in apprehensively.

"How's my little man?" She asked. She hoped he liked the house.

Bentley was dressed in a baggy T-shirt with Captain America's shield on it, and dark sweat pants. He had tennis shoes by the bed and was in only his socks. The bed was pushed against the wall right beside the window. There was a small night table beside the bed with a lamp, his inhalers, and several bottles of prescription medicine. He also had his EpiPen Jr readily available just in case he accidentally came in contact with one of the many items he was allergic to.

His bedspread was covered in Transformers with matching sheets. His hair was unbrushed and he was standing in front of the large window . . . staring.

"How come there are windows only in the front of the house?" Bentley asked, without turning from the window.

Rachel looked perplexed at having an unfinished house. "That's a good question. Hey, did you get a chance to say goodbye to your father?"

He turned his head to her with no expression. "I don't like goodbyes."

She walked up to him and knelt down. She embraced him.

"I can explain about the windows," said Deirdre, who appeared in the doorway without a sound.

Rachel stood up and faced the real estate agent. Bentley looked back out the window.

"It was part of the design by Jacob Reilly," Deirdre continued. "He had a vision of only looking toward the future. His architecture is actually greatly appreciated among his peers."

"Did he ever build anything outside of Lakeshore?" Rachel queried.

Deirdre became noticeably irritated. "Well no, but . . . ."

"But nothing," Rachel interrupted. "I don't like it. It's creepy."

Bentley smiled.

"Well then, I suppose you aren't fond of the dirt floor basement either!" Deirdre snapped.

Rachel got right up in Deirdre's face. "What the hell are you talking about? What dirt floor?"

Deirdre smiled. "If you would have taken a tour of your house before you purchased it, you might know all about it."

"No! I didn't know anything about a what?" Rachel blurted. "A dirt floor in the basement? We'll cover that right away! Where's Jason?"

"I'm right behind you," he said. He appeared as quietly as Deirdre had.

"Damn it!" Rachel screamed. "I will not have everyone sneaking around my house!"

"You were looking for me?" Jason responded. "Maybe that saved you the time you would have spent searching the house. I would like to say that getting rid of the dirt floor in the basement would be really bad. For one thing, you would reduce the value of the house. For another thing, by adding cement or some other compound to the basement, you're going to have to restructure the entire basement. The room is set up with the insulation and wiring to support that part of the house. If you change the flooring now, you'll have to rewire the kitchen and a good part of the living room. It could take months."

Rachel glared at Jason, wondering if he was being honest about the work needed. "Fine," she said reluctantly. "We'll keep the damn dirt floor."

Bentley gave his mother a dirty look. "Mom, damn is a bad word."

Jason smiled at him. Bentley winked at Jason.

Jason and Deirdre decided to leave before anything else was determined to be outdated or not good enough for the new owner.

"Nice move, Jason." Deirdre tried to contain her laughter.

"Oh, you liked that, huh?" He responded. "I'm not letting that bitch destroy the integrity of this house, especially since she didn't have the balls to check it out before she bought it. Cute kid though."

Deirdre stopped walking. "Wait a damn minute! How the hell did you know about the Hagglers buying the house sight unseen?"

"You have your sources. I have mine," Jason concluded.

Eight

April 13, 2014 7:14pm

The two first floor bedrooms were given to Alexandra the maid and Chef Enwain DeDaure. The moving crew had successfully moved all the furniture and essentials. They unpacked and installed all of the appliances by 6:30pm.

After spending almost an hour arguing with Chef DeDaure about the lack of space, among other things in the kitchen, Rachel needed some time for herself. Bentley was content with reading in his room, but there was one piece of unfinished business the new owner forgot all about.

Rachel had her bottled water and iPod as she entered the business office on the second floor. She dressed in her workout shorts and a half-shirt. She put on her best tennis shoes, but wore no socks. She also put her hair into a ponytail.

She figured she was close enough to Bentley's room if he needed anything. She set the time and elevation on her treadmill. She put the headphones on and programmed eight Katy Perry songs on repeat.

Rachel started to jog on the treadmill as she entered her own world. She was unaware she was being watched. Rachel had her back to the bathroom. Her stalker remained hidden in the second floor bathroom as she continued to run.

Twenty minutes later she started to sweat, but continued her pace. The stalker moved a little closer to get a better view.

The stalker could see the open door that led to the second floor landing from the business office,and saw a small figure run past the door. Rachel seemed oblivious to the figure.

Again, the figure ran past the door. It was almost a blur,but it appeared to be wearing something red.

The stalker moved unseen from the bathroom to the landing using the bathroom door. It stood parallel to the wall of the business office.

About twenty to thirty feet away, a small girl stood by the main door of the office. She faced the stalker. Her hair was long and matted. She wore no shoes and her feet were filthy. She was in a torn red dress. She slowly raised her right arm and pointed right at the stalker.

Then she screamed. It wasn't like anything human. The scream sounded like it came from a tormented animal.

The stalker ran into the bathroom again as Rachel pulled off her earphones and ran out the door where the stalker first saw the little girl.

"Bentley!" Rachel screamed.

The stalker returned to its spot when it saw the screaming little girl. Bentley stood in the same spot, facing the same direction.

Rachel embraced her son and tried to comfort him. "Bentley, baby! Are you okay? What happened?"

Bentley glared over his mother's shoulder at the stalker with no emotion. "Mom," he said softly. "That man was watching you."

Rachel turned around to see Jason standing by the bathroom door. Jason looked nervous. "Uh . . . yeah. I was watching you."

Rachel stormed toward Jason. "What the hell is your problem? You scared the shit out of my son!"

"Well, I'm sure he appreciates that kind of language," Jason said, sarcastically.

"Get out of my house!" Rachel screamed.

"Look. Wait-a-minute. I was only watching you because you never got with me about me being your handy man. Hey, I've been here for a while waiting for you." Jason hoped she would believe him. He glared at Bentley who wouldn't stop staring at him. "Is Bentley an only child?"

"What?" Rachel was caught off guard with his question. "What the hell? Yes, he is."

"Does any of the staff have any children here?" Jason insisted on asking.

Rachel tried to figure him out. "No other children are allowed to live here. There are no children visiting either. You're not good around children. Are you?"

"You're not hiring me to be a babysitter," he replied, confidently. "All I want is room and board and something to eat. You don't have to pay me. I'll take care of all of the maintenance. Just pay for parts and supplies and I'll take care of the rest."

She put her hands on her hips still trying to figure Jason out. "Room and board includes something to eat. So, were you really watching me?"

Jason glared at the now smiling Bentley, and smiled back. "Of course I was. I'm sorry for the creepy stalking thing. But hey . . . let's face it . . . you're hot."

Rachel smiled as she started to walk her son back to his room. "Yeah, I am. Haha! You can bunk in the room next to Bentley. Don't bother him. And don't ask me for a key to the house." She disappeared around the corner.

Jason pulled out a lot of keys on a large key ring from his pocket. Don't worry. I won't ask you for a key.

Nine

April 13, 2014   10:47pm.

Jason was wide awake as he lay on the twin bed in the room he occupied. He left his door open so he could monitor the activity on the stairs. The landing was dark except for a hall light that was on by the office. and some illumination from the first floor. He had on a pair of pajama bottoms but no shirt.

He couldn't get the thought of Rachel on the treadmill out of his mind. He also couldn't get the vision of the little girl in the red dress out of his thoughts. Was it his imagination . . . or something else?

Jason didn't have time to ponder those questions because he heard voices coming from the room next door.

Bentley's room.

He had a feeling that being next to Bentley would not be the best place to be in the long run. The kid was creepy.

Jason placed his ear to the wall to hear what was going on with Bentley. He heard a muffled conversation with laughter in the mix.

He felt strange spying on a child, but his curiosity was sparked. *Doesn't that brat sleep?*

Jason walked through his open door and peeked in the direction of Bentley's room. It was completely dark in the hallway that led to the opposite side of the office. Bentley's door was closed, so Jason walked to the other end of the hallway and noticed two bulbs had burned out. That explained the darkness.

More work. *Great.*

Near the end of the long hallway, he could see a dim light coming from the bathroom on the right. He turned his attention back to Bentley's room. There was a faint light coming from underneath the door. He pressed his ear hard against the door.

Bentley's voice could barely be heard through the oak door. "Thank you. No. Haha! That's silly! I don't have any brothers or sisters. You do? Really? My dad's never around. My mom's pretty cool. Yes, she does love me."

"No. You don't scare me."

Jason panicked as he grabbed the doorknob and thrusted the door open. He stood in the open doorway, scanning the room for

Bentley's friend. No one was there. He did notice the closet door was open. He peered over the bed and saw a pillow and a sheet set up on the floor of the closet, as if Bentley had someone sleeping over.

Jason tried to contain his trepidation as he looked the room over. "Hey kiddo. I heard you talking. You know, it's normal to have imaginary friends."

Bentley looked into the closet and started to laugh. "Haha! He thinks your imaginary!"

Jason froze and glared at the closet, but saw no one. That was ridiculous! He's just a kid playing games!

Jason started to gain control over himself again as he chuckled nervously. "Nice. Real funny kid. Oh, hi in the closet! What's your name?" He asked sarcastically.

A breeze blew passed him when he heard a low raspy voice say, "Katie."

Ten

April 14, 2014 8:22am.

"What the hell's going on, Sheriff?" Jason yelled, as he pounded his fist on Artie Donovan's desk.

"That's enough!" The sheriff responded, while trying to remain calm. "You knew the risks! Why is this any surprise?"

"It's that real estate bitch! Isn't it?" Jason huffed. "She's doing this to make me crazy!"

"Stop it!" the sheriff yelled. "It's time you started taking responsibility for your own actions Jason."

Jason lowered his voice. "Stop calling me that! Who do you think it is, if it's not your former bed buddy?"

The sheriff got right up into Jason's face. "First of all, you need to control your mouth! Second, just because you know what happened between Deirdre and I, doesn't give you the right to bring it up any time you want! In case you've forgotten, I'm your only friend here. And I'm the only one who knows your secret."

Jason glared out of the large bay window in the sheriff's office. He started to calm down, because for the most part, the sheriff was right. "Yeah. Look, I'm sorry about bringing up the affair. That was wrong of me. I'm frustrated, because…"

"…you think you're seeing Katie Elkton running around the house," interrupted Sheriff Donovan. "You don't get it, Jason. Or should I call you Griffin?"

"That's my name. Griffin Elkton. The boy who lost his entire family in one night."

The sheriff put a hand on Jason/Griffin's shoulder. "I was the first officer on the scene that night. I'll never forget it as long as I live, but know that I have done everything in my power to protect your real identity. If people knew…hell, if Deirdre knew that you are an Elkton, she would have exploited that for the sake of the tour and who knows what else she had planned."

"See, Artie? You know she's a bitch!" Griffin scowled.

A concerned look crept over the sheriff's face. "I wouldn't go that far Griff. I would say she's an opportunist."

A tear fell down Griffin's cheek against his will. "I saw Katie, damn it! I can't hide how that affects me. She was the only one in my piece of shit family that I cared about. She never hurt anyone! Do you have any idea what it's like to see her...*like that?*"

"No," replied the sheriff. "I can honestly say I have never gone through what you think you're going through. It's the first time that you've been back in that house since..." He trailed off, not wanting to bring any more bad memories back.

Griffin plopped down on an old metal chair with torn padding. He was no longer able to stop the tears. "That's why I didn't want anyone to know I came back as myself. I don't want pity Artie. I don't want the whole, *'oh the poor boy. What can we possibly do for you to make you feel better?'* Nothing Artie! There's nothing anyone can do to take away my pain! If it wasn't for my father beating the shit out of us on a daily basis, we might have made it. Then he started to hit Katie for no fucking reason. Then there was my weak mother. She claimed she loved us, but did nothing to try to get us help. Hell, even putting us up for adoption would have been better than going through what we went through!"

The sheriff did his best to try to be supportive, in spite of the fact that he didn't know where to begin. "That was 20 years ago, Griff. There comes a point in time…"

Griffin's anger came back. "I swear Artie, if you tell me I have to get passed this, I'll break something! I have been carrying it with me and will continue to do so until I die. Maybe a little after that too, I don't know."

"You don't think that maybe you're seeing Katie now, because it's the first time you've been back in that house since she died?" The sheriff finally got to complete his previous thought.

"Hell no!" Griffin replied, with a fury. "I have been cleaning that house for a while now. I've been down in that damned basement a hundred times keeping everything nice and tidy for the stupid tours. I only started seeing her yesterday. I saw her twice…I think."

The sheriff looked confused. "Well, that was the day the Hagglers moved in."

Griffin glared at the sheriff. "Don't think that fact hasn't crossed my mind."

April 14, 2014 9:45am.

Deirdre had just finished getting dressed in jeans and a comfortable top. Skye was typing furiously on the computer. Her mother walked up to her. "Skye, dear?"

Skye was dressed as she always was, mostly in black accented by extremely dark eye shadow. If she heard her mother, she made no attempt to recognize that fact.

"Skye?" Deirdre repeated. "I have an open schedule today, so I thought we could go shopping."

Skye stopped typing. "Together?"

Deirdre laughed. "Of course together, silly. I thought this would be a great opportunity for us to bond."

She had Skye's complete attention. Skye turned to her mother with a questioned look. "What's the scam?"

"What? Why does everything I do have to be a scam of some sorts?" Deirdre huffed. Her tone was off. Something was up.

Skye stood up and faced her mother. "So, you're telling me you honestly want to just take me out shopping? No strings attached? You're so full of shit."

"Hey! Young lady, you will talk to me with respect, even if you don't have any!" Deirdre was livid and thought twice about even wanting to be around her daughter. She grabbed her purse and headed out the front door. She knew trying to bond with Skye wasn't going to work. Her frustration caused her to tear up. She knew she wasn't the best mother, but when she tried, she got the door slammed shut in her face.

Deirdre started the engine and threw it into reverse. She started to wipe the tears from her eyes as she slowly backed up. She looked into the rearview mirror and saw Skye standing behind the car.

Deirdre slammed on the brakes, putting the car in park and exited the vehicle. "What the hell do you think you're doing? You could have gotten yourself killed!"

Skye rolled her eyes. "If you really want to take me shopping, I could use some more nail polish. Maybe a pair of Ugg boots too since you're buying."

Deirdre fumed as she got back into the driver's seat. Skye got into the passenger side. "Wow! We better watch out or people will think we're a real family!" Skye laughed as the car screeched out of the driveway.

***

Deirdre either took a different route to the mall, or shopping wasn't going to be their first stop. Skye looked suspiciously at her mother. She decided to stay quiet until she had proof that there was a detour.

As soon as Deirdre turned onto Sedgewood Drive, Skye knew. She gave her mother an angered look. "What the hell?" Skye yelled. "Why didn't you tell me we were going to this freak show?"

"Hey young lady," Deirdre barked. "I warned you about your swear words! I'm just stopping for a moment. I have to talk to the Hagglers and make sure they got moved in okay."

"You mean kiss their asses!" Skye scoffed.

"You don't have to go in," her mother continued. "However, if you keep talking like that, I will turn this car around and take you home! Oh shit! I've become my mother!"

Skye managed a chuckle as her mother smiled and pulled into the Haggler's driveway. Deirdre got out of the car. "Last chance to see Katie's ghost."

"I'm sure I'll get more chances. Have fun!" Skye finished, sarcastically.

"Suit yourself," Deirdre responded. "I'm leaving my purse here so you know I won't be long. Then it's off to shop!"

As Deirdre walked up to the front door, Skye looked up at the house and got a chill. She watched as her mother knocked on the front door, soon to be greeted by Rachel. They exchanged a few words and Rachel waved to

Skye. Skye waved back with a fake smile. *Bet those boobs are fake.*

Deirdre and Rachel disappeared into the house as the front door closed behind them. Skye looked with curiosity at the house again and decided it probably couldn't hurt to get out and look at the outside.

When Skye got out of the car she felt a stronger chill. There didn't appear to be anything out of place, except for the constant feeling that someone was watching her.

She slowly made her way up the pathway to the front door, while she looked around for any surprises. The chill turned to a real feeling of dread as she stopped about five feet from the door. She clenched her fists as she breathed rapidly. She was transfixed on the door and was gripped by a paralyzing fear. Skye tried to call for her mother, but all she could do was mouth the words.

The front door slowly opened all the way. Skye let out a deep breath, she could move once the door opened. She looked in the house and could see no one around the door who might have opened it. Suddenly, a strong hot wind came from inside of the house and knocked Skye down on the lawn. She jumped up immediately and shook from fright. She stumbled backward as far away from the door as possible. She ended up on the sidewalk by the mailbox. Skye tried to understand what had just happened, to no avail. She crossed her arms, because in spite of the hot wind, she was freezing. She felt someone watching her again. She looked up to the second floor and saw Bentley standing in the window. He didn't move.

He was just staring.

Her breathing became shallower as she noticed it was so cold she could see her breath.

"Fuck this shit," Skye mumbled under her breath, as she ran back to the car. Once inside, she pulled out her cell phone and rapidly dialed her mother's number. "Come on! Come on!" she said, quietly as she stared up at the house.

Skye heard the click of her mother's phone being answered. She didn't give her any time to answer. "Let's go now!" She yelled into the phone.

There was static. Then Skye heard a voice. It sounded like a little girl.

"Griff and Katie went in the closet,

to hide from a big baddy.

Mommy got hurt and so did Griff,

by a monster inside Daddy."

Skye froze expressionless.

"I need someone who will play with me. Won't you come inside…Skye?"

Skye glared at the house expecting to see something or *someone* looking for her as her breathing became erratic.

Then, in a deep, almost demonic voice, Skye heard, *"Play with me, bitch!"*

***

Deirdre said her goodbyes to Rachel Haggler and headed back to her car. She looked around and saw that Skye wasn't in the passenger seat. She looked around the front yard and then looked up at the second floor windows. She saw nothing out of the ordinary.

Deirdre started to get upset. She knew Skye wanted nothing to do with that house. Maybe that was her way of getting back at her mother. She was probably sitting somewhere laughing about getting one over on her mom. She would have to start disciplining Skye. There's no way that she would be allowed to think that she's in control. The mother in Deirdre finally started to come out.

Deirdre got into the driver's side and started up the car, as she thought of punishments that might actually work against her little Hellion. Maybe she would take away her cell phone. Skye was glued to her phone. She even took it to bed with her. Deirdre didn't know Skye's friends, if she had any, but she knew she cherished that phone.

She looked at the passenger seat and realized that Skye's punishment would have to wait.

In the middle of the seat was Skye's cell phone and Deirdre's purse was gone.

Eleven

May 2, 2014   2:14pm

Deirdre stared at her phone. She believed that Skye was taken, in spite of her best efforts to convince Lakeshore's finest. Sheriff Artie Donovan stood over Deirdre as she slumped on her sofa. Female Deputy Alana Sachs accompanied him when he would make a house call to Deirdre, which was every day since Skye turned up missing.

Sheriff Donovan crouched down and placed one hand on Deirdre's shoulder. "Deirdre. I know you don't want to hear it again, but we kind of ruled out kidnapping about a week and a half ago."

"Kind of ruled out, Artie?' Deirdre scoffed. "Why? Is it because no one has come out and demanded anything yet? Is it because you've told me over and over again in so many words that my daughter is irresponsible and left on her own?"

Deirdre burst into tears as Sheriff Donovan stood up. "I'm only saying that Lakeshore has never had a kidnapping, but we have had plenty of kids just running off until they're ready to come home."

Deirdre was frantic. "She left her phone you imbecile! She never goes anywhere without it!"

"The good news is your purse was taken too," Deputy Sachs added.

Deirdre glared at the deputy. "*That's* good news. Is it?"

"Well, what I mean ma'am was that there's been no activity on your credit cards. If anyone took Skye and your purse, we're sure they would have used the cards."

"There was an envelope with over $1,200 in cash," Deirdre rebutted. "I was going to deposit it before Skye and I went shopping. We've discussed this before."

Deputy Sachs regretted her statement. "I'm sorry Ms. Hallsey. I wasn't part of the first responders. I was just trying..."

"To rehash things we've covered," Deirdre interrupted. "If there's no kidnapping then why do I constantly get the pleasure of the sheriff's department keeping me company?"

Sheriff Donovan glanced at Deputy Sachs, then back at Deirdre. "It's because we don't want you going out by yourself and getting into trouble."

Deirdre stood up and faced the sheriff. She gritted her teeth. "I assure you Sheriff, I will not be the one getting into trouble. Just do your damn job and find my daughter."

***

Griffin didn't understand why the Katie sightings stopped with the disappearance of the Hallsey girl, but it was a blessing to him.

He couldn't get the image of the little girl out of his head. He still believed Deirdre Hallsey was somehow behind it in an attempt to convince the new owners that their house was haunted.

As he laid in bed in the room that used to belong to him, he did everything in his power to avoid contact with Bentley next door. *There was something creepy about that kid.*

The fact that Deirdre would involve a sick child in her games made him even angrier. He made it a habit to keep his door closed, stay to himself, and only peek out once in a while when

Rachel was on the treadmill. He made his rounds to ensure that the house was operational and without need of maintenance. The other houses kept him busy most of the week for general preventive maintenance.

Griffin loved his solitude, but he realized it was time to check the basement again.

There was a loud knock on his door, just as he was getting ready to do a quality check in the basement. He sighed and hesitantly opened the door.

Anderson Haggler stood there with a concerned look. "I'm sorry for bothering you, Jason. I won't keep you long. May I have a word with you?"

Griffin raised his brow and tightened his lips. "You're paying my salary, so it's your dime. What's on your mind chief?"

Anderson stepped in and closed the door behind him. Griffin immediately thought that he was in some kind of trouble, so he decided to try to alleviate any tension. "I hope you're not planning on sexually harassing me, because I'm not really into dudes. I am flattered though."

Anderson's expression didn't change. "Cute. I need to ask you a favor that doesn't involve any increase in pay."

Griffin saw his chance to make an impression with his employer. He figured it couldn't be too big of a favor, because Anderson obviously knew how busy he was all day. "I'm your man. What do you need?"

"I need you to watch my wife," Anderson responded, as Griffin tried to contain his smile. "I'm sorry. That's not what I meant to say." Anderson seemed distracted. "What I meant to say is I would appreciate it if you could keep an eye out for Rachel and Bentley. I won't be around much, which is actually par for the course for me. I thought they would be safe in town the size of Lakeshore, but when that girl disappeared right in front of our house…"

He appeared to get lost in his thoughts, so Griffin decided to play the hero. "Hey, I know what you're trying to say. I get it. New place. Weird stuff going on in your front yard. Yeah. I'll keep an eye out for the kid…*uh*…your child and your wife. You can count on me Mr. Haggler."

Haggler's disorientation seemed to increase.

"Thank you. I knew I could count on you."

"Mr. Anderson?" Griffin asked. "Are you okay? I mean you look like you might not be feeling too good."

Anderson forced a smile. "Thank you for your concern. It's hard sometimes to differentiate between ass kissing and real sympathy. Once people know how much I'm worth, everyone wants to be my friend. Do you want to be my friend Jason?"

Griffin didn't know how to answer that. He thought he was being verbally led into a trap, so he smiled awkwardly and shrugged his shoulders.

Anderson laughed and placed a hand on Griffin's shoulder. "Haha! Good job! I believe that you're the first person to make an honest attempt at *not* answering. I knew I came to the right person."

Griffin joined in the laughter. "Well, I am an honest guy."

Anderson stopped laughing and focused on Griffin. "We all lie, Jason. Some are little white lies and some are so big that we have to keep lying to cover the first lie. My wife is attractive. I've seen you looking at her. I don't mind men looking at her. You just make sure that the only undressing you do of Rachel is with your eyes. I am the most powerful man you will ever know. Just because we're in Lakeshore doesn't mean that my reach isn't expansive. Keep your eyes and *nothing else* on my family. If you do a good job, there could be some kind of reward in it for you. If you drop the ball, however…"

Anderson left his thought incomplete for a reason. He wanted Griffin to fill in the blanks. "Do we understand each other Jason?"

Griffin turned serious. "Yes, sir."

"Good," Anderson replied. "I'll check in with you in a couple of days. I have some business to attend…elsewhere."

Griffin nodded as Anderson left his room. He kept thinking about what his employer said about Rachel. Griffin thought back to when he was a child. He remembered that the more his father told him to stay away from something, the more he wanted it.

He was no different as an adult.

Twelve

May 2, 2014   8:16pm.

Alexandra had just cleaned off the dinner table. She had constantly complained that the dining room was too small. The fact that it was part of the kitchen didn't help. Chef DeDaure also complained about his limited kitchen space to really prepare meals the way they were meant to be prepared.

All of that fell on deaf ears. Rachel allowed them to gripe and just smiled whenever she heard enough.

Rachel started to walk her son upstairs when she noticed that Griffin was following them. "Your stalking is getting more reckless, Jason."

Griffin tried to look serious as he stared at her body. "I'm just trying to be a bigger asset to you and your husband. You're paying me pretty good and I thought I should help out more with Bentley."

Rachel showed honest surprise. "Seriously? I believe this is just another way for you to try to catch a glimpse of me, but if you're serious…" She crouched down and faced Bentley. "Honey? Do you mind if Jason takes you to your room? I'll be up later to tuck you in." She kissed his head while never taking her eyes off of Griffin.

"It's okay Mama," Bentley responded. "He's funny." Bentley laughed a little before coughing.

Rachel stood up and pushed out her chest toward Griffin. "Alright, Jason. Be my guest and earn your pay. Be careful with my son. He's all I have."

"Well you have a husband too," Griffin added, with an air of sarcasm.

Rachel ignored him as they reached the second floor landing. She headed for her bedroom as Griffin escorted Bentley to his room. Bentley walked into his room as Griffin stood out in the hall for an extra moment. He could see into Rachel's bedroom since she conveniently left the door wide open. She looked at him and removed her blouse. She then turned her back to him and removed her bra and smiled, while she headed to her bathroom.

Someday bitch.

Griffin entered Bentley's room with a look of frustration. Bentley looked up at his new caretaker.

"You like my mom," Bentley said.

Griffin looked toward her bedroom. "Your mom is…something else."

"I like you Griff," Bentley blurted out.

Griffin turned to Bentley in complete surprise. *Had the sheriff somehow spread the word about who he was?* His heart raced as he tried to force a smile. He closed the door as he did everything in his power to play it off like Bentley was crazy. *Yeah that's perfect. Making it out like an 8 year old is insane.* "Wha…where did you hear that name?"

Bentley laughed intermittently with coughing as he jumped up and down on his bed.

"Hey! Stop that!" Griffin shouted. "I promised your mom I'd take care of you!"

Bentley immediately stopped laughing and dropped to his knees on the bed. He looked like he was in pain as he held his chest. "Ouch." He exclaimed.

Griffin went up to him. "Are you okay? Can I get you anything?"

"No, thank you," Bentley responded, politely. "Sometimes it hurts. Sometimes I have to stop and rest."

Griffin started to calm down, but still had an important question for Bentley. "Why don't you lie down Bentley?"

"I have to change for bed first. You can't expect me to sleep in my clothes, silly. Haha!" Bentley had a burst of energy as he jumped off the bed and headed for his closet. He started to change into his pajamas. Griffin looked out the window and noticed it had started to rain. He thought he saw someone standing across the street looking at the Haggler house. He squinted and was able to make out a figure in a hoodie standing unaffected by the downpour.

The figure didn't move. *Maybe it was a creepy lawn jockey.*

Bentley's giggling drew Griffin's attention back into the room. He saw the child standing in the closet looking at one of the walls and laughing. Griffin could feel a cold chill go up his spine.

"I know!" Bentley squealed with delight. "He thinks I don't know. I don't know if he'll believe you."

Griffin froze until the eerie supposed one-sided conversation was over. "Was...that your friend, Bentley?"

Bentley came out of the closet with his pajamas on. He jumped into bed and pulled the covers up to his chest. "Yep! She's the one who told me who you are."

Griffin felt a panic wash over him. He had thought that *Bentley's friend* had disappeared the same time that Skye Hallsey did. He had hoped that there was a connection. "Have you been talking to your friend all this time?"

"Every day," Bentley replied, confidently.

Griffin gulped. "Where is she now?"

"In the closet," Bentley replied, nonchalantly. "She doesn't like to come out, especially when she hears arguments."

Just like Katie used to be.

Griffin gritted his teeth and refused to believe any of it. "You know Bentley. It's not nice to lie. Your friend doesn't really exist. Does she? You're getting your information from Sheriff Donovan. Aren't you?"

Bentley looked confused. "I didn't lie. You did. Your name's Griffin Elkton. You tried to help Katie after her accident. She knows that." Bentley's expression turned serious. "She knows everything."

"That's bullshit!" Griffin yelled, as he punched the wall.

The door flew open. Rachel stood there extremely pissed off. "What the hell, Jason? You couldn't even handle this small task of helping my son get ready for bed?"

Griffin's anger increased. "I don't care what you say, but that little shit of yours better answer my questions…"

Rachel didn't give Griffin a chance to finish his sentence. She tightened her fist and punched Griffin square in the jaw. He reeled backward out into the hall.

"Use a gun Mommy!" yelled Bentley.

Rachel turned in surprise to look at her son as she was then lifted off the ground by some unseen force and thrown into the same wall that Griffin punched. She slid to the floor and jumped up shaking. She stared at her son while her bottom lip quivered in fear.

"She really doesn't like violence, Mom," was all Bentley said.

May 2, 2014 8:16pm.

Rain was in the forecast for Lakeshore. The lone figure stood their ground across the street from 2782 Sedgewood Drive. They made no point to hide or try to be sneaky.

The figure didn't care about that.

All they did was watch the house. Their eyes would move from one end of the outside of the house back to the other end. The figure looked carefully at each window for movement or *something else.*

The figure was dressed in a gray hoodie with the hood pulled up. It concealed as much of the figure's face as possible. They had on a fanny pack, black sweat pants, and tennis shoes in case they had to run.

The figure had but one thing on their mind…to see something odd happen. Even if that meant standing in the rain.

The dark clouds let out a few drops to let Lakeshore know that every once in a while the weatherman got it right.

No one was usually out that late for anything. It was late for Lakeshore. Everything shut down about 7pm and then it was time at home for the residents.

The figure knew that if they waited long enough they would see something. *Anything.*

After a short while, the figure saw movement through the window at the far right of the house on the second floor. *Bentley's room.*

That's where they saw the most activity. This night was no different.

As the rain started to come down harder, the figure saw a man looking out the window. The man looked out the window as he leaned closer. The figure knew that he could see them.

The figure didn't care.

After the man disappeared into the room, the figure moved closer to the house. They crossed the street and stood on the sidewalk directly in front of the house.

A few more moments and the figure heard yelling coming from the same room, followed by a loud thump. The figure stood mesmerized and waited for what happened next.

A half hour later, the light went out in the room. The rain let up enough to show anyone clearly who stood at the window. The figure stared into the window as if they expected another show to begin. They weren't disappointed as an eerie red light appeared in the room.

Bentley appeared at the window and looked straight at the figure. He looked like he was in a trance. He stood there for several minutes. The figure felt a chill, other than being in the rain. They could almost make out someone standing beside or behind the child. All they could see were the piercing red eyes that glared at the figure.

The figure pulled the hoodie down. It was Skye Hallsey. She looked at the presence beside Bentley. "It's not over asshole," she said under her breath. "I know who you are. Come and get me."

She stuck her middle finger out toward the window with pride and turned to walk away.

Thirteen

May 2, 2014   9:56pm

Deputy Alana Sachs brushed her blonde bangs out of her eyes as she wrote down the incidents as they were described to her by Rachel Haggler and Griffin Elkton. Of course, Griffin was under the guise of handyman Jason Kellogg. Deputy Sachs was in her mid-20s and one of the best officers that Lakeshore had to offer. She had straight cut hair and soft brown eyes. Her smile was genuine and made people think of her more as a friendly store clerk than a representative of the law.

Rachel, Griffin, and Sheriff Donovan sat at the dining room table, while the deputy stood next to Rachel. Alexandra had made coffee for whoever wanted it.

Alexandra had been with the Hagglers for twelve years. She was always trusted to watch Bentley and take special care of Anderson. She felt left out since Anderson was gone most of the time. She did enjoy working with Bentley and Rachel though.

Over the years she had gained weight and didn't move as fast as she did before. She was in her late 40s and was more than happy to remain with the Hagglers as long as she could still clean. She kept her shoulder length brown hair tied in a bun in case she had to help the chef with any food matters.

The more people that she could care for, the better she liked it. Her brother Adrian was married and his wife was pregnant when Alexandra left Greece. When she was a young girl of 21 years, she had two miscarriages in her native city of Patras, Greece. She later got her Work Visa and moved to the States. One thing led to another and she ended up working for the Haggler family.

She loved taking care of children and was a little put off when Rachel Haggler asked Griffin/Jason to watch Bentley. No matter what happened, she was the most loyal employee the Hagglers had.

"Would anyone like a nice bowl of Lobster Bisque?" Alexandra asked, quietly. "We have some left over from dinner and it's always just as good the second time around."

Sheriff Donovan hadn't eaten since lunch and the thought of *anything* sounded good. "If you don't mind my deputy and I will be more than happy to try your bisque."

Deputy Sachs looked questioningly at her boss. "I already had a Tuna Melt before we came over."

The sheriff leaned over to her. "I know that, skinny. Maybe at my age I need a little extra to keep me going." He placed his hands on his stomach and grinned. She nodded and chuckled to herself.

Alexandra went into the kitchen and pulled out the pot of leftovers from the refrigerator. She placed it on the stove top and took the lid off.

Deputy Sachs looked at the sheriff. He nodded and smiled as he took a sip of his coffee. "Alright Mrs. Haggler. I need to ask you about what happened here tonight. Please tell us everything that happened once you went into your son's room."

Rachel glared at Griffin. "That son-of-a-bitch called my son a *little shit!*" She tried to contain her anger, because of everyone present.

Griffin looked at the sheriff, as Artie raised his eyebrows. "I didn't call him a...okay, maybe I did," Griffin replied, as the sheriff lowered his head. "I didn't mean it, but… he was freaking me out with talk of his little invisible friend."

"His friend?" Deputy Sachs responded. "I take it this friend is imaginary?"

Griffin laughed. "Maybe you better ask Mrs. Haggler about that." He gulped down some coffee.

Rachel stood up unwilling to contain her anger. "I will keep my voice down only because Bentley is sleeping upstairs."

Alexandra lit the fire under the pot. She kept the lid off as she looked in the fridge for other things to add.

Rachel placed her hands on the table and directed her anger at Griffin. "You not only called my son a *shit*, but then you had the nerve to throw me out of his room. By force!"

Griffin looked at the surprise expressions on the sheriff and deputy's faces. He stood up, spilling his coffee. "Hey! Wait just a damn minute! You knocked *me* out of the room! Whatever happened after that…"

"You lying bastard," Rachel interrupted. "Keep your voice down, you prick. You threw me out of Bentley's room right after he begged me to use a gun on you."

"Whoa there," the sheriff butted in. "What the hell is going on here? You two need to settle down before we take you to the station under more controlled circumstances."

Alexandra cleaned the fridge door while trying to hear the argument. Unbeknownst to anyone, a pool of red liquid collected on the ceiling directly above the open pot.

Rachel and Griffin sat down against their will. They decided that they would rather settle their differences in the house.

Anderson ran into the dining room which startled everyone. "What's going on here? Can't I stay away for more than a few hours before something insane happens?"

His anger was also directed at Griffin, who rolled his eyes at being everyone's target.

The red substance on the ceiling dripped drop by drop into the open pot of bisque.

"Mr. Haggler, could you please calm down," Sheriff Donovan said, as he tried to maintain some control.

"Calm down?" Anderson responded, while the veins in his neck pulsed and throbbed. "When I got the call from Rachel about this shit…"

Rachel grabbed her husband's arm. "Honey? I didn't call you."

"Are you calling me a liar?" he bellowed. "That's it! I'm going to have to do something to make sure I'm here all the time!"

Rachel looked confused as she tried again to calm down her enraged husband. "I never called you. I don't know why…"

"Yeah!" Griffin interrupted. "Just like I didn't throw you anywhere!"

Anderson looked at Griffin. He walked over to him and pushed him out of his chair. Griffin fell to the ground but bounced up to his feet quickly. He was shaking as he started to back up. Anderson pursued.

It was the sheriff's turn to leave his seat as he tried to intercept Anderson.

A slow, thin stream of red liquid dripped into the pot at a faster pace.

Anderson got to Griffin first, who had just so happened to be standing in front of the open door to the basement. Anderson pushed him backward. Griffin stumbled backward as visions of 20 years ago flashed through his mind. The look of terror on his face would be something Rachel would never forget.

Griffin lost his footing and proceeded to fall backward into the basement. He tumbled a few times. He could hear the old wood creak and snap several times before he hit the soft dirt floor. He hoped that the snapping sounds he heard on the way down all belonged to the wooden steps.

Anderson followed Griffin into the basement as everyone tried to stop him. As the head of the household stopped in the middle of the basement stairs, he looked back at everyone crowded into the small door opening. Deputy Sachs drew her weapon.

That's when the basement door slammed shut leaving Anderson and Griffin alone.

Fourteen

May 2, 2014   10:32pm

Anderson's head slowly turned to face Griffin, who was on his feet and grateful that he didn't break anything that he knew of. Anderson took the steps slowly down to Griffin. As he made his way closer, Anderson's eyes turned a dark blood red. The moonlight was all the light they had, but Griffin could make out Anderson's silhouette.

"You want to fuck my wife, don't you?" Anderson asked. He had a softer tone than Griffin expected.

"Dude. That's your wife," was all Griffin could respond with.

"Don't fuck with my son...asshole." Anderson glared at Griffin.

Griffin was more than nervous. "Look, I don't know what the hell's going on, but I think you need like a swear jar or something. I would never do anything to your son. He's a cool kid. I like Bentley. Things just got out of hand. I never tossed your wife anywhere though."

"I know," Anderson answered, as he brushed off Griffin's shoulders. "I know what happened."

"You don't look so good," Griffin exclaimed, as he glared at the red eyes. "So who told you what happened? Bentley?"

"Katie," Anderson replied, as he passed out and hit the floor.

***

Anderson was stretched out on the living room sofa, while Rachel and Deputy Sachs stayed close by. He had a cold compress on his head as he started to recover.

Sheriff Donovan sat with Griffin on the stairway that led to the second floor. "What's going on Griffin? I can't get a straight answer out of anybody in this crazy house."

Griffin was still shaking from his earlier experience. "Crazy house is right on the money! I don't know what's going on, but I know that I didn't push, pull, or do anything to Rachel

Haggler. I haven't touched her at all. Not only that, but why is the *man of the house* being babied? I'm the one who practically broke his neck falling down the stairs!"

The sheriff saw Griffin's eyes plead with him, as Alexandra came up with two bowls of hot bisque. "Pardon me Sheriff and Mr....*uh*...Jason, but I have plenty of bisque. I know you wanted a bowl or two, Sheriff." She smiled as she held out both bowls.

"No thank you, Alexandra. I appreciate it, but I seemed to have lost my appetite," the sheriff responded while he glared at Griffin.

She nodded and went into the living room. Anderson was now sitting up rubbing his neck. Deputy Sachs was just finished writing as Alexandra approached with a big smile on her face. "Forgive me Mr. and Mrs. Haggler, but I have some wonderful Lobster Bisque and Sheriff Donovan isn't hungry anymore. It would be a shame to throw it out. It's not any good after the second reheat. The chef told me that."

Deputy Sachs smelled the bisque. "You know what? I would love to try it. Would it be possible if you could wrap that up to go?"

Alexandra smiled as she was about to offer the second bowl to Rachel.

"Both," said the deputy forcefully, yet respectfully. "I could eat both. I'm sorry. I don't get to eat like this a lot. If it's no trouble?"

Alexandra looked at Rachel for approval. "I don't care. Give her the whole damn pot. I can't stand leftovers anyway." She glared at Anderson. "Are we done here?"

"I'm done," the deputy added, as she followed Alexandra to the kitchen.

Rachel waited until they were out of view before she spoke again. "Why don't you believe me? Jason has to leave!"

Anderson stood up and faced his wife. "You're a lying bitch and you know it!"

Rachel stepped back in surprise. "Wha...what the hell are you saying?"

"Don't play coy with me, Rachel," Anderson continued. "You've always liked to flirt! You can get away with a lot more now that we're in this hell hole! Hey! Don't worry about it! I'm a lying bastard!"

"I…don't understand," she replied. She was genuinely shocked. "Why are you saying these things to me…*now?*

Anderson lowered his head as if he was in pain. "Look. I've been under a lot of pressure right now. I've got a migraine that I just can't shake and things aren't working for me outside of this house. *Hell*, they're not working for me inside the house either! I just…need some time to sort everything out. The move. The fact that I…"

"Stop it!" Rachel interrupted. She was in tears. "I know things haven't been the same since the cabin, but we promised to work things out!" Rachel had a pained expression as she started to wring her hands.

He placed his arms around her. "You know what happened at the cabin. We were on our way to healing our family and then, *it* happened. You know that's why I stay away as long as I do. I still love you Rachel, but we need time and some extreme circumstances to get back together."

Rachel held on to Anderson tightly. "I'm sorry."

"Don't apologize," he said, calmly. "I'm the one who cheated and you're apologizing. Haha! Just try to see to the future. I don't see a problem with Jason. I have a feeling he will be a valuable asset. You must get passed this thing with him as well. You're a smart girl. You can use what you have at your disposal to keep him in line. When the chips are down, I believe he will do what he has to." He smiled as he kissed her.

She stared at Griffin.

***

The sheriff stood up and stretched. "Don't get old, Griff…Jason."

Griffin was nervous. "What the hell is that supposed to mean? Am I supposed to die before I get all fat and old like you? And watch it with the name thing."

The sheriff looked around to make sure no one over heard them. "It's a good thing you dropped the charges against Mr. Haggler. You need to be here. On the inside."

"What the hell are you taking about?" Griffin rebutted. "On the inside? You know there's some shit going on. Don't you?"

The sheriff looked concerned. "I'm not saying that there *isn't* anything going on, but I think it would be best for all of us if you stayed here. You need to behave so you can have a look around."

Griffin slapped his forehead and laughed. "You know there's something going on and *I'm* the one who has to play detective? You got a lot of balls Artie."

"Jason please," the sheriff pleaded. "We have a 15 year old girl missing and a houseful of lunatics whose stories don't correspond with each other's. All I know is what I've been told. You told me that Deirdre is messing with you by bringing up Katie. Mrs. Haggler said you threw her into the wall. I examined her and she has some bruising on her back. You say she's nuts and then her husband gets pissed off at you and pushes you…"

"Threw," Griffin interrupted.

"Threw you down the stairs," the sheriff continued. "About two weeks ago a teenage girl disappeared and here's the funny part, Jason. You told me that all of this weirdness happened since the Hagglers moved in. I know who you really are, so I kind of feel sorry for you."

"Spit it out, Artie," Griffin said, as he grimaced.

Sheriff Donovan took a deep breath. "Okay. I'm going to level with you. I have protected you until now, because I remember that little boy who lost his entire family in one night. There's only so much I can do to cover your ass. Aside from all of the testimony about everything that has happened, I have to look at the legal implications and the things that can be proven. I don't know why they want you to stay here, but that's not my job to know. If I didn't know you, I would say that you are nothing but a trouble maker! I would advise you to keep your distance from Mrs. Haggler while you're trying to figure out how to be a good employee.

"Dude! She's hot!" responded Griffin. He was oblivious to everything else the sheriff had said. He then lowered his head. "I know how it looks. I'm not an undercover cop, am I?"

"No, you're not," replied the sullen Sheriff. "Consider yourself under house arrest."

"Son of a bitch!" yelled Griffin.

Rachel and Anderson looked over. "Everything alright Sheriff?" She asked.

Sheriff Donovan waved at her. "You have to be careful, Jason. I can't protect you anymore."

Deputy Sachs came out with a couple of plastic bags that each had some weight to them. She had a Cheshire grin. "Are we all done here Sheriff?"

The sheriff smiled back and then gave a stern look to Griffin while pointing his index finger at him. "Yes, we're all done." He walked to the living room. "I just wanted to let you both know that we have finished with our investigation. Thank you for your patience and hospitality."

"Not a problem Sheriff," Anderson said calmly. "I will go up to say goodnight to my son and then I too, must be on my way. Rachel has your number if she needs anything."

"Yes, she does," the sheriff replied, while glaring at Griffin. "She has my cell phone number too. Just in case.

Fifteen

May 3, 2014 8:45am

Mayor Jonathan Sutton just arrived at his office, prepared for another calm day in Lakeshore.   At least that's what he had recently…several calm and peaceful days. That day, however, would prove to be anything but…

He had just placed his lunch on the far edge of his desk and sat down on his favorite chair. After he sat down, he would close his eyes and get into a positive mood for the day, just in case he had to deal with anything out of the ordinary. Mayor Sutton always liked to think he was prepared for anything.

He wasn't prepared for his first visitor though. Skye Hallsey was escorted in by his secretary, Gloria. "I'm sorry for bringing this up first thing, Mayor, but guess who showed up after all this time."

Mayor Sutton tried to be polite, but couldn't resist a sarcastic jab now and then. "I can see Ms. Hallsey there, Gloria. Thank you for bringing her in."

"I just didn't know if you would see her without an appointment," she replied.

He sighed. "I appreciate the concern, but I like to believe I have expressed my open door policy to the residents of Lakeshore several times before. I do love your attention to detail though. There's no O.C.D. in you."

Gloria grimaced. "A.D.H.D. Mayor. A.D.H.D."

Gloria left with a chip on her shoulder as Mayor Sutton pointed to an empty chair. Skye sat down. Her demeanor was quiet and reserved. He pulled a small bottle of orange juice out of his lunch bag. "Would you care for something, Skye?"

She was caught off guard by the non-chalant way he treated her reappearance. She might have thought that everyone would react the way that she knew her mother was going to. His non-judgmental way to everything, made him approachable. "No thank you Mayor. I would like to talk to you about a problem."

He smiled as he took a gulp of his juice. "I usually don't get involved in matters of the family, if I can help it, Skye. I do know the name of a good family counselor, if you'd…"

"It's the Haggler place," she interrupted.

The Haggler place…*again.* He put his juice down and lost his smile. He tried to be as polite as possible, without showing his frustration with the matter. "Let me guess. Katie Elkton has made an appearance."

Skye became annoyed at his attitude. "I don't think you realize the implications of what's going on in that house. You need to have the sheriff or some people who follow ghosts to investigate. This is a serious situation, Mayor."

Mayor Sutton thought for a few moments before he responded. He was still Lakeshore's voice of reason, no matter what kind of malarkey came into his office. "The fact that the situation seems serious enough for you to come out of hiding, tells me that I *should* do something. Even if it isn't my area of expertise. I can contact your mother if you want."

'I'm on my way there now," Skye replied, without showing any emotion. "I'm sure she'll be *thrilled* to see me."

Skye left his office as he thought about how articulate that young woman was. He knew she was smart, he just wished that she didn't always dress like she was going to a funeral.

Mayor Sutton picked up the phone and dialed for an outside line. Once he heard the dial tone, he proceeded to dial a number he thought he had forgotten. "Yes…hello. I'm sorry for bothering you at this hour. I know…I could use your help. Yes…the town will take care of your bill. Great! I'll see you in an hour then."

May 3, 2014   9:57am

A tall thin man entered the mayor's office. He had a Bluetooth device in his right ear and wore thin wire-framed glasses. He had a short brown hair cut an inch over his ears. It was greased with a little bit of a duck tail in the back. His skin was pale, but smooth. He always wore a suit with the pant legs four inches too short. His ties were always different colors and they were thin and appeared to be made out of rope. He always carried a notebook with him wherever he went, just in case he had to write down something. His name was Dr. Samuel Constance. He had a doctorate in psychiatry and had been the only practicing therapist that Lakeshore had known in quite some time. He had a distinct Jeff Goldblum quality about him and despite his introverted appearance, he always sparked up conversations with everyone he could.

"Well good morning to you, Mr. Mayor," he said, with a slight pitchiness in his voice. "It's been a long time. Four years and twelve days, right?"

The mayor forced a smile because he knew what he was about to ask would cause an almost immediate backlash. "You're always right. I've admired your photographic memory, Sam."

"Eidetic, Jonathan," Sam answered, with an almost condescending tone. "I have an eidetic memory. It's a common misconception. The often used, but non-existent term 'photographic memory' is a misnomer. Just like the term affiliated with that movie, Total Recall."

Mayor Sutton took a deep breath. "Sam. I called you because I believe we have a situation in Lakeshore concerning a possible case of either mass hysteria or even the power of suggestion."

Sam started to shake his finger at the mayor. "No, no, no, Jonathan. I appreciate the fact that you are interested in solving a problem, but to diagnose a potential psychological phenomena prematurely could lead to all kinds of ramifications, the least of which is following the wrong course of action to proceed for treatment. I love you like a brother and a friend, Jonathan, but I beg...no *implore* you to leave this to someone in the field of which I have dedicated most of my life studying."

Mayor Sutton didn't want to excite his friend more and didn't have time to decipher all of Sam's psychological mumbo jumbo, so he decided to cut to the chase. "Sam. The address is 2782 Sedgewood Drive. There have been reports by three different individuals of seeing the ghost of a young girl who died accidentally there 20 years ago. Since then Deirdre Hallsey has made a career out of making people think that Katie Elkton is haunting the house. Can you help out?"

Sam leaned back, tilted his head to the side, and sported a Cheshire grin. "It would be my ultimate pleasure, Jonathan. My ultimate pleasure."

May 3, 2014   10:18am

Deirdre Hallsey rushed out of her house, already late for her appointment with a potential real estate client. She had her car keys out, as she stopped short a few feet from her vehicle. Skye was leaning against the driver's side door with her head lowered and her mother's purse in her hands.

Deirdre fought her emotions. She felt anger for Skye's blatant lack of respect. Then she felt relief just knowing that her daughter was alright. She knew Skye. If she started to discipline her daughter, it would fall on deaf ears. Skye was her own young woman, despite her age.

"I'm going to be late for an appointment, Skye," Deirdre said, without hesitation. "There's lasagna in the fridge. You'll have to warm it up. Be careful because the microwave still has a problem when you program it for more than three minutes. Your phone is in your room on your bed."

Deirdre grabbed her purse from her daughter, got into the driver's side, and started the engine. Skye slowly moved away from the car. The vehicle screeched out of the driveway. As Deirdre drove away, she looked at her daughter in the rearview mirror and started to cry uncontrollably.

Skye stuck her hands in her pockets and walked slowly toward the house, kicking small rocks off of the driveway. "It's okay Mom. I'm fine," she said out loud as she went into the house and closed the door.

May 3, 2014   2:47pm

A totally restored 1941 Plymouth Woody Station Wagon pulled up into the driveway at 2782 Sedgewood Drive, right next to Rachel's Escalade.

The Woody was Sam's pride. He even restored it himself. He chose the Mahogany wood for the paneling and carefully chose the varnish to accent the natural look of the wood. He exited his work of art, as he smiled and let out a sigh. He then grabbed his briefcase, pulled the car cover from the passenger side, and meticulously covered his car. He headed for the sidewalk that led to the Haggler's house. When he arrived, he made a disgusted face at the doorbell. *How many germ infested fingers have touched this?*

He placed rubber gloves on both hands and proceeded to knock loudly. He stepped back about three feet, so as not to be right in the face of whoever answered the door. He hated when people did that. It especially happened with solicitors.

The door opened to reveal Alexandra. She had a smile and raised her brow as if she expected a sales pitch of some kind from the tall, lanky stranger.

"Good afternoon madam," Sam said with a gleam in his eye. "Is the lady of the house in?"

Alexandra had gotten rid of more solicitors and Jehovah's Witnesses than she had years on the earth. She knew every verbal trick of the trade to keep their spiel as short as possible. "I'm sorry sir, but there are only college students here. Perhaps another time. Thank you."

As the door started to close, Sam stuck his brown loafer in to prevent the door from closing completely. "Please tell Mrs. Haggler that Dr. Samuel Constance is here at the request of our honorable Mayor Jonathan Sutton."

Sixteen

May 3, 2014   3:15pm

Sam sat with perfect posture on the sofa in the living room. Alexandra had prepared him a cup of Green Tea with one half a slice of lemon and an exact teaspoon of cinnamon. He has taken his tea like that for as long as he could remember. Sam was not a big fan of change and always had a bit of an ego about him when it came to being able to control his surroundings.

His ego was about to be tested.

Rachel entered the living room like a pissed off runway model. She wore a loose fitting white summer dress with a floral print. She was barefoot and her hair cascaded down her shoulders, like a shimmering black waterfall. Her discontent at having to entertain someone the mayor sent without checking with her first irritated her beyond description.

She assumed she could entice him visually and then send him on his way. That method had worked ever since she was aware of her sexuality.

Sam stood up out of respect as Rachel stopped in front of him. "Good afternoon, Mrs. Haggler. I appreciate you seeing me without so much as an invitation. I do apologize for the intrusion."

Rachel put her hands on her hips. It was almost as if she were sending a signal to him about who was in charge. "I only allowed you in because the mayor sent you. I don't know why he needed an errand boy, but I can assure you…I don't bite."

Sam chuckled. "I would never question anything to do with your oral abilities, Mrs. Haggler. I'm sure that would be more of an interest to your dentist of choice. Please allow me to introduce myself before I disclose the purpose of my visit."

Rachel gave Sam a confused look, then nodded.

"Thank you," Sam said, as he straightened his tie. "I am Dr. Samuel Constance. I understand that there is great concern among several members of your household that there might be a little girl wandering around post-mortem."

"Try speaking in English, doctor," Rachel huffed.

"My apologies again, Mrs. Haggler, but I was," he replied with an air of condescension. "I was told that a little girl has been visiting you. A little *dead* girl?"

Rachel's patience was almost at an end. "Are you making fun of me?"

"Oh my, no!" Sam replied. "It has been my profession to never label or put down those who are oblivious to my command over the English language."

His comment appeared to attack, although he was sincere.

"Our time here is done," Rachel said angrily.

"Finished," Sam corrected.

Rachel no longer suppressed her anger. "What did you just say?"

Sam realized that if he was to be of any help, he needed to diffuse a potentially hostile situation. After all, that's what he did. "I'm here to get rid of your ghost, Mrs. Haggler."

Her anger was almost immediately replaced by curiosity.

May 3, 2014   3:36pm

Deputy Alana Sachs skipped lunch because of the cramps she had all that morning. She had kept a regular menstrual cycle and knew she wasn't due for another week and a half. For the first time in several months, she passed on the morning doughnut.

Sheriff Donovan noticed the slower movements with his *usually* energetic deputy. He waited to see if whatever she was going through would pass before he said anything. As he approached her desk, he noticed that she was pressing against her stomach. "Sachs. Are you alright?"

"Oh. Hi Sheriff," she responded. It was more than apparent that she was in pain. "You know, that's the question of the day. I started feeling weird late last night. I had a lot of trouble sleeping too, but now I'm getting a little concerned myself."

"You need to go home, or better yet, go to the doctor," Sheriff Donovan replied, with concern in his voice.

Deputy Sachs let out a huge burp. "Oh crap! I'm sorry, Sheriff. For some reason I have a lot of gas. I just hope it doesn't come out the other end."

"Well, if it does, you'll need to be prepared for it," he responded, while trying not to think about her last statement. "Your shift is almost over anyway. As your boss, I insist that you go to the doctor first. It might be a contagious bug. If I get sick, that would ruin my five year record." The sheriff laughed.

"Thank boss," replied Deputy Sachs. "I'll go straight to the doctor." She got up slowly as she continued to press on her stomach.

"Why do you press on your stomach like that Sachs?" He asked.

She burped again. "Sorry. If I ever felt nauseous or had cramps as a kid, my mom told me to always push my stomach in as much as I could stand. She said whatever was in there would then be forced to come out one way or another."

Sheriff Donovan held his nose. "If your burps are that potent, I don't want to hang around to see what happens from the other end. I think you should go now."

She ran out and tried to cover her embarrassment.

***

Griffin walked past the living room and into the kitchen to fix himself a snack. He saw the mysterious stranger in the living room talking with Rachel. Her dress may not have had the desired effect on Sam, but the same couldn't be said about Griffin.

Rachel stood with her back to him as he quietly entered the living room. Alexandra had just given Sam another Green Tea and was going out the door that led to the kitchen.

"Hey Alex!" Griffin yelled, as Alexandra turned around. "Sandwich please! Corn beef on rye with lots of mustard and a pickle spear! Thanks!"

Alexandra went into the kitchen as Rachel walked up to Griffin. "You better remember one thing, Jason!" Rachel yelled. "You're part of the hired help! In fact, Alexandra is more a part of the family than the staff, so you will treat her with the same respect that you treat me!"

Griffin smirked. "So, I'm supposed to lust after her too?"

Rachel saw Sam out of the corner of her eye. He leaned toward her and Griffin, while writing frantically on a legal notepad. "Oh please, don't stop on my account. We can go into these issues once we've covered the *dead girl* sighting first."

Griffin had a surprised look for Rachel. "Who the hell is this guy?"

"Dr. Samuel Constance, at your service," Sam replied, while nodding his head.

"He's here because we have a dead little girl who can't seem to find her way back home," she said, sarcastically.

"Hey!" replied Griffin. "Don't ever make light of dead children running around!"

Sam smiled as he squinted his eyes at Griffin.

"I, myself, have not seen anything strange," Rachel said, nonchalantly.

Griffin was losing his patience. "What? What about when you got thrown into the wall?"

"You did that!" Rachel barked back.

Sam stood up in frustration. "Please, please. As rewarding as this is professionally, I really must insist we address one psychosis at a time. If I am to explore the Katie Elkton situation, I need detailed statements from both of you and the third party who had an experience as well."

Rachel glared at Sam. I don't know anything about a third party. Maybe Bentley? I already told you, I didn't have any experiences with anyone dead that I'm aware of."

"Who is this Bentley?" Sam responded, politely.

Rachel looked up toward Bentley's room. "I don't think he knows anything."

"I think he better talk to the doc," Griffin said quietly, while he gritted his teeth.

"No!" Rachel bellowed. "He just a child! He's not going to be put through the third degree! He's been through enough!"

"A child?" Sam asked, while grimacing. "No, no, no. That will not do at all. I make it a practice not to involve children in my therapy."

"Good!" Rachel said, triumphantly.

"It's because children are extremely unreliable when being interviewed, especially where their parents are concerned," Sam continued. "I have an aversion to all things children, so that is definitely out of the question."

Rachel turned to Sam. "What? What is that supposed to mean?"

Sam smiled slightly. "I mean no offense to you or your child. I'm sure he's a wonderful little...*rascal*. There are millions of people who cherish and would even go so far as to wish for a little one of their own, but I find that in dealing with the eventual adults, they are easily distracted and have a tendency to be easily manipulated by said parents."

"What about adults?" Griffin added. "Adults lie all the time?"

"Good point!" Sam said, as he pointed with approval at Griffin. "That's what makes it so fun for me. I do believe one should enjoy one's work, no matter the profession. I have spent my work...nay, my life, dedicated to the human psyche. I have had several papers published and I dare say, I have made a huge splash in the world of psychiatry. I have analyzed adults from afar and from special studies. One can really see the true nature of people in their natural environment, where they are relaxed and feel a sense of security. When they come to my office, they are guarded from the start. They have ample opportunity to prepare themselves mentally for me in one way or another. When I come to one's home, they are already relaxed and feel no need to hide or pretend with me. I am but a guest in their sanctuary and offer no threat. I had opportunities to move my practice, but I find that the people who reside within the larger cities, have practice with hiding from society in one form or another. They are experts in avoiding the issues that they consider too personal."

Sam had Rachel and Griffin's complete attention as Alexandra replaced his teacup with a fresh one.. He smiled and nodded at her as he continued, "Forgive my rambling."

"So what is all of that supposed to mean, doc?" Griffin asked, as if he already knew the answer.

"It means, my dear boy, that I know when people are lying or hiding something."

"I obviously don't need to be a part of this, because I didn't see anything, so I'm going to check on my child," Rachel said, almost defiantly.

Sam crossed his hands in front of him. "Just the fact you have allowed me into your home, tells me that although you may not believe in Katie's ghost, you do believe something needs my expertise. I thank you for your silent vote of confidence."

Rachel left the two men alone. Sam turned to Griffin. "I don't believe in ghosts, but I do know that you knew the little girl in question, simply by your reaction to Mrs. Haggler. Would you care to elaborate?"

Seventeen

May 3, 2014   7:28pm

Deputy Alana Sachs didn't want to be in the hospital. When her doctor couldn't find anything wrong with her, in spite of her vomiting, he had no choice but to send her to Lakeshore Memorial.

She hated hospitals. When she was a little girl, she went to the hospital only three times. The first time was when she was four. Her grandmother went in with heart issues. When she was six, her grandfather went in with a collapsed lung. When she was nine, she went into a hospital for the final time as a child because her mother had suffered a severe head trauma in a car accident. Deputy Sachs lucked out that day because she was supposed to be riding with her mother to the store. She had a fever of 103 and couldn't go anywhere.

All three hospital visits ended the same way. Each of her family members never left.

She remembered her mother as if she never left. She was an attorney in Lakeshore. The Sachs family was a generational one that never seemed to leave the small community.

She looked up to her mother and wanted to be an attorney as well, but after she was in an accident caused by a drunk driver, Alana chose a different path. One in which she could try to make a difference before anything got to trial.

A *pre-emptive strike,* she called it.

Alana's father was a good man, but he had no ambition. After several failed business ventures wasting thousands of dollars that his wife brought in, he decided to be a househusband and never did anything involving risk again.

Alana was never close to her father anyway, but after her mother died, they grew even further apart.

Alana graduated the academy in the top 3%. She memorized the code book and loved her job. She preferred not to have a partner. She didn't want to be responsible for anyone and vice versa. She knew her mother would be proud of her.

She was extremely personable and had many friends in and out of the Sheriff's Department.

There was another reason for her not wanting a partner. Sometimes, she didn't exactly follow the law. Occasionally, she took matters into her own hands. Especially where drunk drivers were concerned. There were never any drunk drivers who survived a car accident, but only if she was the first one on the scene.

She made sure she was first, on as many of the calls as she got. The accidents increased during the winter months. Mostly during tourist season.

She took the risks her father would never take and she administered the justice that her mother was too honor bound to administer.

As she laid in her hospital bed waiting for the results of various tests that were run earlier, she contemplated what could be wrong with her. She hadn't been sick since she had the flu which possibly saved her life when she was a little girl. She wondered what the test results would prove, if anything. *What if it's a rare disease that had no cure?*

With her mind racing through all of the scenarios, she kept going back to the only thing she really feared.

Alana Sachs was afraid of dying alone.

May 3, 2014   10:45pm

Rachel watched from the doorway as Bentley slept soundly. She smiled at how peaceful her son looked. Her smile disappeared as she glared toward the closet, wondering what really happened the night she was thrown into the wall. Her memories had never failed her before, or so she thought.

As a child, she remembered her mother telling her she had an overactive imagination. Rachel's world always had to revolve around her. When it didn't in the real world, she would make sure it did in her mind. Within the deep reaches of her mind, she could do no wrong. Even when she got caught setting fire to an empty doghouse, she denied it was her. So much so, that her father almost believed her, in spite of the fact that he was the one who caught her doing it.

Rachel was definitely a daddy's girl.

She realized at an early age how to manipulate the opposite sex to get what she wanted. Although that fact alone, didn't seem unusual for a young girl, Rachel took the art of manipulation to a new level.

She always got what she wanted because her parents were wealthy. She never knew or cared how they made their money, as long as it was there. Rachel liked being spoiled, but being able to use what she had to control people, excited her even more. As a child, she would throw a tantrum when accused of something she actually did, but she would still refuse to admit it. She also produced her sad face, which melted her father's heart all of the time.

As she got older and started to fill out physically, she realized the old ways wouldn't work anymore.

She then mastered the art of seduction.

Rachel had found her true calling and power by the age of 16, by simply letting her male acquaintances get what they wanted in return for what she wanted. She actually felt they were being cheated because she always made sure she received much more than they did. She even got so good that sometimes she didn't even have to give them anything but false promises.

Her parents did everything in their power to change Rachel's ways. Her behavior did irrevocable damage to their reputations. They had tried everything to keep their daughter's extracurricular activities under control. They finally came to the point where they had no choice but to disinherit her.

That might have taught young Rachel a hard lesson, if she wasn't already manipulating at least three men at the time. She left home at 17 and never looked back. She didn't care about losing her inheritance, because she felt she was making her own way in the world.

One bedroom at a time.

The fact that she had been as successful as she had been without once taking responsibility for any of her actions, was just another accomplishment she was proud of. She believed her parents should have been proud that she was independent. She proved them wrong. Look at where she was at this point in her life. She had made it. Rachel believed she was a great mother and an amazing wife.

No one was going to take that away from her. She had worked too hard to get where she was to have it taken away.

***

Rachel walked into her bedroom and noticed Anderson was already in bed. He always laid on his side. She smiled. It had been a while since she and her husband had been intimate. She closed the bedroom door behind her and walked to the bed. It didn't matter if he was asleep. *He would wake up for her.*

She stepped out of her summer dress and proceeded to remove her bra and panties. She knew he had always worshipped her body. He couldn't resist her. *Ever.* Even when he cheated on her, Rachel knew he thought of her every time he made love to his secretary. She *knew* it.

She slid under the covers and pressed her body against his back. She heard a slight groan. She nibbled his ear.

"Rachel? Maybe later. Okay?" Anderson said, to her surprise.

She laughed nervously. "What? Come on. You know that's not how this works." She continued to nibble his ear.

Anderson turned on his other side to face her. He looked upset. "Welcome to the new, *this*". What's your problem Rach? Can't you see I'm tired?"

Rachel recoiled in surprise. "Tired? That's your excuse? Tired? Being tired never stopped you before."

He started to lose his patience with her. "Damn it! You already know what's wrong! It's because you..."

"Me?" She interrupted. "I'm sorry but it's *never* me! I'm a wonderful mother and a faithful wife!"

Anderson's laugh mocked her. "You think you're so damn perfect. Don't you? Little miss 'everything has to go my way'! Do you even care about what I'm going through? I provide for you to go flaunt yourself in front of anyone who will take a look!"

Rachel got out of bed and put on her robe. "Hey! That's not fair! That's what you told me to do!"

"With Jason, yes!" he bellowed, as he started to calm down. "Look. I'm not stupid. I know who I married. I did that for a reason. I didn't want anyone taking me for everything after the first week of marriage. No one in their right mind would have signed all of the pre-nup shit that I had you sign."

Rachel again, was caught completely by surprise. "I signed it all, because I wanted to be with you!"

He got out of bed and walked up to her. "You signed it all, because that's how you operate. There isn't anything you wouldn't do to get what you want. We had an understanding. That's why I signed you up."

After all of the times Rachel had to fake tears to get what she wanted, a real one rolled down her cheek. "Signed me up? You make it sound like you recruited me."

"Is that what you do with whores?" Anderson responded, nonchalantly. "Now if you don't mind, I'd like to get some sleep. I have a killer headache."

Rachel ran crying from her room. She knew it wasn't her fault why her husband acted that way. *It was never her.*

She stood on the second floor landing as she leaned against the rail. She heard a child's laughter coming from the first floor. She immediately ran to Bentley's room and quietly opened the door. He was fast asleep.

She ran through scenarios in her mind that included an extra child in her house. She looked confused as she left her son's room and looked down to the first floor. It was dimly lit, but she could still see a small figure standing in the shadows near the hallway which led to the kitchen.

Rachel ran toward the stairs and stopped suddenly as she felt a chill go down her spine. She took a deep breath and took one step at a time, until she was on the ground floor.

The child's laughter echoed from the hallway where Rachel saw the figure. She walked closer. Surely this was an illusion brought on by all of the talk of this Katie person. *Maybe Dr. Constance was on to something.*

Rachel followed the sound of the child into the hallway. She looked toward the opening to the kitchen. "Alexandra?" Rachel called out. "Chef DeDaure?" No answer.

She had one last name to call out before she ran out of people who she knew for sure *should* be in the house. "Jason?" No answer.

Rachel moved slowly to the darkened kitchen. She had minimal light from the hallway. She stopped at the corner before entering the kitchen. She peeked one eye into the room. It was quiet, except for a dripping sound. It sounded like someone had left a water faucet on just enough to drip.

Rachel's heart was beating extremely fast as her eyes diverted to the kitchen ceiling. She could barely make out some kind of wet spot. Whatever the moisture happened to be was dripping down on to the floor forming, what appeared to be, a large puddle.

Rachel's apprehension and possible fear was replaced by anger. She wanted to know who was to blame for the mess. She entered the kitchen and flipped on the light.

She walked up to the puddle while cursing the names of everyone who had access to the kitchen. She stopped at the liquid and placed her hands over her mouth. *It was blood.*

Her lower lip started to quiver as she stumbled backward. She fell and was pushing herself back with her hands and feet. The basement door was open. Rachel heard child's laughter coming from the basement. "Fuck that!" She exclaimed as she managed to stand to her feet.

She turned to see a little girl about 10 years of age. The girl had long matted hair that hung down in front of her face and was wearing an old red dress. Of what Rachel could see of the girl's face, it had a grayish color to it. There were deep dark circles under the girl's eyes and there was mud caked on her arms and legs.

Rachel stood still for a moment, not knowing what to say. She finally decided it was one of the neighbor's children who had somehow broken into her house. Probably through the basement. "Are your parents...?"

Before Rachel could finish her question, the little girl's mouth opened and a roach crawled out. The roach crawled down her neck and worked its way to her arm. Rachel was sickened and amazed at the same time. She watched the insect as it reached the girl's hand.

Rachel started to slowly back away as she noticed the girl's hands. The fingers were bent and misshapen. The fingernails were about 3 to 4inches long and had yellowed. They were as twisted as her fingers. Her hands looked more like claws. The little girl clawed at Rachel's thigh and started to laugh. Rachel could feel the pain in her right leg. She looked down to see three deep slices. She limped toward the basement and turned around just in time to see the little girl wrap her arms around Rachel's legs.

There was an incredible burning sensation in her legs as she heard gurgling coming from the girl's throat. "You need to be punished. I'll show you how Daddy punished me."

Rachel let out a scream before everything went black.

***

Deputy Sachs woke up to find herself in a strange bed. She wasn't at the hospital anymore and was dressed in her deputy's uniform. She looked around the room and realized she had never seen it before. She knew she was in a king sized bed though. It was extremely comfortable. *No wonder she dozed off.* She got off of the bed as soon as she heard the shower running in the adjoining bathroom.

She checked to make sure she still had her firearm and breathed a sigh of relief when her hand found it on her gun belt. She walked slowly toward the bathroom as the shower was turned off. She noticed the bedroom door was closed, so she decided to go into the bathroom and get some questions answered.

As soon as she stepped into the light from the bathroom she saw a man furiously drying his hair with a towel.

The man was completely naked.

Deputy Sachs tried to recover from her embarrassment to not only admire the physique in front of her, but to compose herself so that she could find out where she was. "Excuse me? Sir?"

"Hello Deputy," replied the man, who continued to towel dry his hair. "Could you do me a favor?"

His voice sounded familiar, but she had a hard time concentrating on it, while she glanced at him every chance she could. "Yes, sir. If you don't mind, could you…tell me who you are?"

The man under the towel laughed. "I'm sorry. I thought you knew where you were. I'm Anderson Haggler."

Deputy Sachs breathed another sigh of relief as she realized she must have been in the Haggler house. "Sure. Okay. What can I do for you, Mr. Haggler?"

"I really need some aspirin." Anderson dropped the towel to the floor. She gasped when she saw his face. Most of the front of his face was missing. The skin looked like it had been ripped apart from the inside out from the bridge of his nose to his neck. Only the back rows of his upper and lower teeth were visible. His chin and nose were gone. His tongue was intact and she could see where it connected to the floor of his mouth. The bloody meat that was exposed, was reminiscent of an antelope's internal organs after a lion had chewed on them for a while. "I have a killer headache," he said. She could see his tongue move with each enunciation.

"How…can you…talk?" She asked, as she started to go into shock.

He dropped the towel which was full of blood, as Alana started to shake her head. She felt nauseous and put one hand over her mouth to prevent the bile from coming up. She glanced down at the floor by the towel and could make out pieces of bone and teeth mixed with blood.

168

She turned and opened the door. She closed it behind her and leaned back against it to catch her breath.

A woman with long black hair ran up to her. She was dressed in a black body suit. "I know what you're going through," she said. Her words almost comforted the deputy. "If you want to get out of this alive, you have to trust me."

Deputy Sachs nodded her head as she forced down more bile. The woman in black led the deputy by hand to the ground floor. That's when Alana realized where she was.

She pulled her hand from the woman and looked around. "What am I doing in the Haggler's house?"

"Are you crazy?" Said the woman. "The man in the room introduced himself as Anderson Haggler. How could you *not* know where you are? I don't have time for games, Alana. Will you follow me, or not?"

Deputy Sachs nodded again as the woman again grabbed her hand and led her into the kitchen. The basement door was open. The woman let go of the deputy's hand and ran toward the basement. When she got to the open doorway, she tripped on a turned up piece of tile and plummeted down into the darkness of the basement.

A young boy ran up to the basement doorway and cried out, "Rachel! No!" He then proceeded to follow the woman into the black.

Deputy Sachs breathed heavily as she slowly approached the stairs that led down. She stood at the open doorway and could see a figure huddled by the bottom stair. There was just enough light to see a man hunched over *something*.

The man was sobbing. He mumbled at first and then the deputy could make out what he kept repeating. "All the king's horses and all the king's men...couldn't put Katie together again." The man turned to look at the deputy.

It was Griffin.

He disappeared into the darkness of the basement leaving a lone figure standing by the bottom stair. It appeared to be a little girl.

Deputy Sachs saw the girl in a red dress. Her hair was matted and she was covered in mud and dirt. Her long black hair covered her face. There was a wheezing coming from the girl as her head started to rise. The deputy could see the girl's face was disfigured. Her lower jawbone was only connected to the left side of her face. She tried to take a step forward. Deputy Sachs heard bones cracking and breaking with each movement by the girl.

The girl tilted her head slightly to one side. Deputy Sachs heard skin slowly rip from flesh as blood started to pour out from the girl's neck.

The deputy had seen enough. She ran toward the front door. Once she got there, it wouldn't open. She tried every door on the first floor to no avail. They were all sealed shut.

She looked upstairs hoping that's where her salvation was. As she ran up the stairs, she could hear wheezing coming from downstairs. She got to the second floor landing and looked around, unsure where to go. The wheezing got louder.

She heard a child's voice call to her. "Deputy! It's safe in here!" It was Bentley. He was leaning out of the doorway to his bedroom.

Deputy Sachs ran for all it was worth as the wheezing became even louder. It seemed like it was right near her ears. She tried to block it out as she finally made it to Bentley's room. She ran inside and grabbed the door with both hands. She pushed the door closed. When it was closed, she pressed her face against it and started to cry. "You're not getting me, you son of a bitch!" She laughed as she heard a splashing sound under her feet as if she had just stepped in a small pool of water.

She looked down at her feet. She was standing in blood. She kept her eyes focused on the bloody floor as she turned around and away from the door.

The room was completely devoid of furniture and the entire floor was cover in blood. There were constant drips of the red liquid originating from the middle of the room.

Deputy Sachs panicked as she saw Bentley Haggler on what appeared to be a bloody swing. His hands gripped tightly to each *rope* of the swing as he pumped his legs and swung back and forth. He looked fine except for the fact that he wasn't in color. In fact, the only color she could see in the room was red.

172

Bentley smiled at Deputy Sachs and said,

"Griff and Katie went in the closet,

to hide from a big baddy.

Mommy got hurt and so did Griff,

by a monster inside of Daddy."

Bentley started to laugh as blood continued to drip from a place higher than where he was. The deputy noticed that the blood was coming from the ceiling. Her eyes followed the bloody ropes up.

She saw a naked woman with long black hair who was melted onto the ceiling. The skin on most of her back, elbows, and ankles looked like it was fused to the ceiling to keep her from falling. Her skin stretched with the weight of her body. The woman's stomach appeared to be torn wide open. From the gaping wound, her intestines were stretched out almost to the floor.

Deputy Sachs realized the ropes that Bentley had been gripping so tightly, *weren't ropes at all.*

The bile was burning the deputy's throat as she could almost see the woman's face. *Rachel Haggler.*

***

The deputy woke up in a cold sweat. She looked around in a panic and vomited immediately all over the floor. She had vomited nothing but blood as her stomach cramps increased.

She wiped her mouth with part of the bed sheet and started to breathe easier once she realized she was still in her hospital room. She was shaking as she pressed the button for a nurse. She had a feeling her nightmare wasn't quite over.

Eighteen

May 8, 2014   12:06pm

Rachel's eyes popped open. She felt fatigued, which was unlike her. She would always wake up with an endless amount of energy. That day was different for some reason.

She dragged herself out of bed. She glanced around and noticed that Anderson wasn't there. *Nothing new there.* She looked at the clock on her nightstand. "Are you shitting me? I never sleep this late!" She realized she was dressed in panties and one of Anderson's night shirts. She wondered if she had been unconscious for their first sexual interaction in a long while. *That would figure.*

She went into the bathroom and looked in the mirror. Her hair was matted and looked like she hadn't washed it in a few days. She took a few sniffs in the air and realized her hair may not have been the only thing that hadn't been washed in days.

The woman who always took great care to look and smell beautiful had slipped up somewhere. Her head was foggy as she loaded her toothbrush. As she brushed her teeth, she pushed her hair out of her face with her free hand. She had huge bags under her eyes.

As she rinsed her toothbrush and set it on the sink, she did her best to remember the last thing she did before she went to bed the night before. She remembered the fight with Anderson. She remembered how horny she was last night. She was even thinking of seducing Griffin. She was stressed and needed some relief.

Surely, there was someone in this Podunk town who could satisfy her. After she cleaned herself up, she would find out.

Her mind was still in a fog when she disrobed and stepped into the shower. *Hot water will hit the spot!*

She turned on the water and waited for the steam to fill the bathroom before she moved. The water pelted her head as she hung it down and placed her hands against the shower wall. She closed her eyes and remembered the fight with Anderson in even more detail. *He was so…different.*

As her aching body was massaged by the pulsating water, her mind started to clear. Her memory went to what happened after the fight. *In the kitchen.*

The kitchen. She assumed it was just a dream, until her right thigh started to burn as the water touched and ran down it. Just her right thigh. She stepped back from the spray and looked down at her thigh. Her mouth dropped as she saw three parallel slice marks. With closer inspection, they definitely looked like claw marks.

Rachel put both of her hands over her mouth to prevent herself from screaming. She shook her head as tears started to fall randomly on her cheeks. She pressed her back against the wall of the shower and slid down to a seated position. The wound had already started to scab. *If a wound this deep occurred just last night, how was that possible?*

After her shower, she towel dried her hair and immediately put peroxide and gauze on the wound. She wrapped an Ace Bandage several times around her thigh to secure the dressing. She secured it with a metal clip and then put on a long yellow dress with a sunflower pattern on it. She knew she wouldn't be able to wear short dresses for a while. She put on lipstick and mascara. Her leg would not prevent her from looking sexy, if she could help it.

As soon as she was finished, she left her hair wet and headed for the closed bedroom door. She stopped short when she heard two male voices on the other side.

***

Anderson was leaning against the railing just outside his bedroom door. Dr. Samuel Constance stood beside him with his pen and notepad ever ready. Sam was dressed almost exactly the way he was on his first visit. He didn't like change.

Anderson was dressed business casual with a black polo shirt that had Haggler Industries sewn over the right breast pocket. He also wore khaki slacks and dark brown shoes. He had a look of concern on his face. "I appreciate you coming back, Dr. Constance. There are definitely some strange things going on here. Unfortunately, I'm not here enough to give you any answers."

Sam straightened his glasses. "Mr. Haggler. You need not make excuses for working and providing for your family. It is an admirable trait. With my help, we can find out what all of the hullabaloo is. I will say that Jason is extremely illusive. I tried to ask him some questions about the mysterious Katie Elkton and he evaded me as simply as a fly would evade my hand in an attempt to swat it."

"Feel free to conduct your interviews at any reasonable time," Anderson responded with a smile. "I would like to be able to feel that my family is being watched by someone who doesn't have the hots for my wife."

Sam laughed. "I assure you, Mr. Haggler that I have no sexual interest in anyone in this house. My interest is purely psychological. I do hope your statement though, was not based on any assumptions of my gender preference."

Anderson smiled. "Not in the least. I noticed you don't glare at her like everyone else does."

Rachel had heard enough. She wasn't one to mince words and was fully prepared to be a part of the conversation. She opened the door and acted surprised to see the two men standing there. "Oh! I'm so sorry for interrupting, but don't stop talking just because I'm here. I'm also so sorry about not being up earlier. I usually don't sleep so soundly. I'm much better now though." She smiled at both men.

"I bet you did get enough sleep, Rach," Anderson said, as he smiled. "You never go out with wet hair. It's nice to see some humanity in there. I didn't expect to see you for *another* four days."

"Another?" She asked, ignoring his comment about her hair. "I only slept about twelve hours!"

Sam backed up a step and started to write on his notepad, which angered Rachel.

"Anderson stood up straight and glared at his wife. You've been asleep for four days, hon."

***

Deputy Sachs woke up screaming. Her heart rate was around 150 as she began to thrash around causing the I.V. to become dislodged from her arm. Two nurses came rushing in to calm her down and get the I.V. back in. She looked extremely pale. Her sudden energy burst was more than enough to drain her. With her fight gone, the nurses were able to reestablish the I.V. connection. Her heart rate slowly returned to normal.

Once the nurses were satisfied that Deputy Sachs wasn't going to hurt herself, they checked and rechecked the E.K.G. One of the nurses approached the visitor who had been witness to all of the commotion. "She should be okay now, Sheriff Donovan," said one nurse. He nodded as she left the room.

He had a dozen Daisies in his hand as he looked at his deputy and wondered if she would ever be fit, not only to return to duty, but to return to her life.

The deputy's eyes remained barely open as her head turned toward the sheriff. "Hey boss," she said weakly. "Have you been here all this time...for me?"

The sheriff forced a smile. "Off and on, Sachs. Actually, a lot of us from the department have been coming here in shifts to make sure you're going to be alright. The nurses told me you've been asleep for a while."

She adjusted herself in the bed. "If you tell me I've been *Rip Van Winkle-ing* it, then I might as well just go back home now."

He put the flowers on the table near her bed. "No. Nothing like that. Look, I'm going to be honest with you. You've been asleep for about four days."

Her eyes teared up as her lower lip quivered. "What the hell's wrong with me, boss?"

His smiled faded as he tried to fight back a tear. "I wish I knew. Hell, the doctors don't even know and they've had you hear for almost a week. They're stumped Sachs and frankly it's starting to piss me off! They even called in some specialist from California."

Deputy Sachs had a hopeful look as she gulped. "Well that sounds promising. Has he been here yet?"

"Been and gone," Sheriff Donovan replied, while the tears started to flow against his will. He shook his head. "They were talking about moving you to a facility in Michigan."

She could no longer hold it together. "Michigan? What the hell is this inside of me?"

"I really don't know," he said, while trying to comfort her. "At least you've been getting some sleep. Maybe the rest…"

"Sleep?" She interrupted. "No! Anything but sleep! Do you have any idea what kind of fucked up things I've been dreaming about? I don't think I ever want to go to sleep again!"

He could see the fear in her. A fear that he'd seen only one other time. The fear was his and it was for a 12 year old boy named Griffin Elkton. He was afraid what would happen to a child who suddenly lost all of his family at once. Deputy Sachs' fear was stronger. Something almost…primal.

"I don't know what to tell you Sachs," he said, while he tried to find anything to tell her so she wouldn't give up. "The doctors said it resembles several illnesses, but can't be treated as any of them. They tried everything. I really believe that they have."

The deputy turned her head in anger. "So what am I supposed to do? Am I supposed to just let this thing consume me while it drives me crazy in my dreams?"

Sheriff Donovan became just as aggravated as his deputy. "I don't have the answers, Sachs!" He stepped back as he felt remorse for his outburst. "I'm sorry. Hell, I thought it was damn food poisoning, since your cramps appeared shortly after you ate the Lobster Bisque from the Haggler's house."

All of a sudden, it was like a blinding, yet all revealing light that appeared in front of the deputy. *Why hadn't I thought of that?*

The Lobster Bisque. It had to be the bisque. The answer was right in front of her the entire time. "Thank you for your concern, Sheriff. I'm sure I'll be just fine. Tell everyone they don't have to babysit me anymore. I'll be leaving the hospital soon."

Her sudden calmness, unsettled the sheriff even more than her hysterics. He would let her have it her way though. She deserved that much respect. "Whatever you want, Sachs. You're a smart girl and I'm sure you'll do the right thing." He bent over, kissed her cheek, and then left the room.

Deputy Sachs knew the sheriff had to be right about the bisque. She had forgotten all about it when the doctors ruled out food poisoning.

The Hagglers.

They had allowed *something* into their bisque. That something was destroying a good officer from the inside out. She gritted her teeth as she remembered all of the times people got away with murder. She felt a rush with every drunk driver that she helped along to the afterlife. She made sure it would be the *last* time they hurt or killed anyone.

It was a job she embraced. Vigilante had always been an ugly word to her. She preferred *champion of the underdog*. She made people safe. Not just for the day, but for as long as she had the power to do so. She felt she probably should have been given some sort of award for her public service. After all, she deserved it.

She had a new target. A target that would have gotten away with it, if it wasn't for her boss. It was as if her boss had given her permission to administer justice to the Hagglers. For the first time since the deputy's cramps started, she had focus. She could feel the need to prevent the Hagglers from poisoning others.

Ever since they, the Hagglers, moved in, it appeared they would never fit into the Lakeshore community. The deputy hid a Smith & Wesson 9mm handgun in her apartment. She acquired the weapon with the filed off serial number from a drug dealer who was just passing through.

The 9mm never made it to the evidence locker.

It would appear that it would be used for the first time since she obtained it. She had waited for the perfect time to break in her new toy. She knew she would have to wait until night before she escaped the hospital. After she picked up her new *friend,* she would pay the Hagglers a visit.

She smiled as she thought about ridding Lakeshore of the trash. *Who knows who they might have killed before?*

***

Rachel sat on the first step leading from the second floor landing. She was almost in the fetal position as she rocked back and forth. Anderson sat next to her with Sam hovering by the railing.

She was frustrated with having slept for four days. "Never in my life have I slept that long. Never."

Anderson put his arm around her. "Here's a thought. Why don't you go see your son? I'm sure he'd like to see his mom after almost a week."

Rachel put one hand to her mouth. "Oh shit! My baby!" She got up and ran to Bentley's room.

Sam looked at Anderson suspiciously. "I believe you have an abnormal fondness of sarcasm, Mr. Haggler. That is not a healthy attitude."

"Shut the fuck up, Doc," Anderson said matter-of-factly. "Psychoanalyze the others, but leave me alone."

***

Rachel opened the door to Bentley's room slowly. She peeked in before she entered the room.

He was lying on his stomach with his blanket covering him. "Mommy? Is that you?"

"Yes, honey," replied Rachel. "I'm so sorry I haven't seen you in the last few days. Mommy hasn't been feeling well." She walked slowly to the bed.

"Mommy?" Bentley repeated. "My tummy hurts."

Rachel perked up and rushed to her son. She threw the covers off and fell backward at the sight of her child's bed.

It was covered in blood.

"Bentley!" she screamed. She grabbed his side and turned him over so he was facing her. Her hands were shaking as she noticed the entire front of his shirt and pants were covered in blood.

"Mommy it hurts," he repeated again.

"Mommy will make it better," she replied, as she started to remove his shirt. She noticed that blood was pouring from two holes. One in his chest and the other in his stomach.

Rachel cried out as she dropped to her knees. She tried frantically to wipe the blood off of her little boy. The more she wiped, the more appeared. She grabbed his blood soaked shirt. It dripped on the floor in her hands as she ran out to the landing. "Anderson! Someone! Help me! Please, my baby!"

She made it to the railing by Griffin's room and collapsed on her knees once more. Griffin opened his door and rushed to Rachel. He arrived just as Anderson and Sam did. She gripped Bentley's bloodied shirt as if her life depended on it.

"Please help my baby," she kept repeating in a soft voice.

Anderson grabbed her by the shoulders. "What's wrong with Bentley? What did you do?"

Sam made a mental note of the fury he saw in Anderson's eyes. He wrote it down as well.

Rachel held up Bentley's shirt. Anderson grabbed it from her and threw it on the floor right beside her.

"What?" he yelled. "What the hell are you trying to tell us?"

Her face was bloated due to her intense crying. She looked up confused at her husband's question. Then she looked down at Bentley's shirt. The same shirt that she practically tore from her child.

The shirt had not a drop of blood on it.

She couldn't explain what had happened. It may have been a simple matter to let those who gathered around her to think she had some residual effects from the four day sleep. If it were anyone but Rachel, that might have been the outcome.

"That…wasn't the shirt…I took from him," she answered, as if she were in a daze. "His…bed. Full of…blood."

The word *blood* instigated the three men to rush toward Bentley's open door. Anderson was the first to arrive. They all entered the room. Rachel looked toward the room expecting to hear groans of anguish from Anderson and gasps of horror from Griffin and Sam. She heard nothing.

She struggled to her feet and stumbled to her son's room. She braced herself against the door frame. She kept her eyes closed. No matter what else happened, she didn't want to see all of that blood again.

"Mommy?" She heard a familiar voice as she slowly opened her eyes. Anderson was sitting on the edge of the bed next to Bentley. Her son was sitting up, holding his stomach. Sam and Griffin stood at the back of the room. They remained quiet. There was one thing missing from that picture.

Blood.

There was absolutely no trace of blood anywhere in the room, let alone in the bed. She rushed to her son and embraced him. Anderson got off the bed and backed up a step.

"Baby!" Rachel cried. "Are you okay?"

"Yes, Mommy," replied Bentley. "But my tummy hurts."

She looked at her shirtless son. No blood. No holes. "I'll get you something for your tummy baby. Where's all the blood?"

Anderson grabbed her and practically dragged her out of the room. Once they were on the landing, he turned her to face him. "What the hell is your problem?" Anderson commanded. "What kind of thing is that to ask your son?"

"But I saw…" Rachel replied as if in a haze.

Anderson dragged her over to the shirt she had brought out. "Look at it! Damn it! Look at it!"

She picked up the shirt and looked it over. "No blood." She started to cry again.

Sam left the child's room leaving Griffin in there alone with Bentley. "You better not do anything weird," said Griffin to the child right before Sam closed the door. Sam made a note of the comment and followed the married couple, but kept his distance.

Rachel looked like an emotional wreck. It was obvious to Sam, she had really believed that she saw what she said she saw. He needed to hear more before he could make any diagnosis.

Rachel looked confused as Anderson faced her. "Four days asleep! Waking up at noon! What's going on? Are you cheating on me?"

That appeared to wake her out of her stupor. "What? You told me to cheat on you! What the hell is wrong with you? You called me a whore!"

"Oh come on Rach! Let's call a sheep a sheep. Shall we?" He responded.

She stood without his help. "I used to know what you wanted! You cheated on me with that bitch! I told you that you could do anything at all, except fuck somebody without me being around! That was the one deal breaker and you still had to test the water! I don't know you anymore!"

"You know what?" Anderson replied, as his anger increased. "Fuck anyone you want! In fact, you can pick from the fine specimens here in Lakeshore!"

Rachel hit his chest with both hands simultaneously. "Damn you to hell! We were supposed to work things out at the cabin! You told me we could work things out!"

Sam inched closer and listened intently.

Anderson breathed heavily as his anger increased. "The cabin? Always the damn cabin! *Let's all go to the cabin and fix things!* Hah! Fix things, Rach? Do you know how you fixed things?"

Rachel let her arms hang behind her back to prevent her from hitting Anderson. "How *I* fixed things? Maybe you should have told me you *impregnated* your secretary before you decided to patch things up with me!"

Anderson's anger appeared to vanish with that statement. He couldn't look his wife in the face. "When did you find out? I made sure…"

"You made sure no one knew outside of your secretary and you," Rachel interrupted. She started to calm down, once she realized she had the upper hand. "You didn't know what happened after I caught you two in your office. I approached her the following day and had real deep heart to heart with her. I made her a deal after I found out about the possible new heir to *my* fortune. I didn't care what she did with the brat as long as she signed a contract that I had our attorney draw up. It stated she was in no way to demand, extract, blackmail, or accept any money in any way. She was also never to mention that *it* was yours. In return I set up a college fund for the little bastard and I gave her one million dollars tax free. Our attorney thought it was also in your best interest to do it this way, so he kept his mouth shut as well."

Anderson glared at Rachel. "That explains why she quit a week after you caught us. I thought it was because she was embarrassed to be caught."

Rachel glared right back. "Don't tell me that I had no right. I had *every* right. I protected my family and my child from this nightmare. I knew it would have come back to haunt us...eventually."

"You never forgave me though," he said.

"You never told me of your own free will," she replied with a Cheshire grin. "Would you have forgiven me?"

"You had no right to do what you did," Anderson said, accusingly.

Rachel laughed. "I already told you I had every right to do what I did."

Anderson tried a more sincere approach. "I took two months off of work to rebuild this family."

Rachel placed her hands on her hips in defiance. "Yeah. How did that work out for you? What has it been, almost a month? You're still going to work. Every time you come back here, you say something about all the work you're doing."

Sam was close enough to see Anderson's expression turn serious. "You know what I'm doing, Rachel. You know exactly what I'm doing."

Rachel smiled as if she had caught him in another lie. "Oh, and please tell me what exactly you do when you leave here."

"Work," he said reluctantly, as he walked back to the bedroom.

Sam's peripheral vision caught a young child in a red dress running on the first floor. He saw her go into the bathroom. "I must take my leave, but before I go…a question. Do you have a daughter as well as a son?"

Rachel shook her head.

"Perhaps a neighbor's little scamp then?" He inquired.

"No," Rachel replied. "We just have Bentley."

"Then off I go," he responded, while trying to ignore what he saw. He chalked it up to a momentary mental weakness while obviously succumbing to the power of suggestion. He removed it from his thoughts.

Sam focused on something he hadn't heard enough of. There was something mysterious about the cabin that the Hagglers kept talking about. There was also a heavy dose of stress about whether or not Anderson Haggler was working when he left their house. Either way, Sam felt it was his responsibility to get to the bottom of those issues. After all, he couldn't help the family if he didn't know everything he needed to know.

Bentley's bedroom door opened and an angry Griffin came out. As he brushed by the Hagglers, he said, "Great parents you are. The kid said his stomach hurt. I'll get the medicine. I know where it is."

Nineteen

May 8, 2014   7:46pm

Chef DeDaure was creating a culinary masterpiece. He had every burner on the stove working, because he sensed the tension in the house and wanted to fill the air with the smells he was most fond of.

Chef Enwain DeDaure was born and raised in a little town in France called La Rochelle. He was born to a French father and a Welsh mother. It was his mother who named him after her father. The spelling was different, so instead of being Enwayne like his grandfather, he became Enwain, which was more accepted by the French.

Enwain looked like his mother's side of the family. He was blonde and had blue eyes. As he got older, he wanted to make a statement in the cooking world, so he dyed his hair white. He never went back.

He had an amazing ability to paint from memory, which is what his father wanted him to do. He decided along the way, that cooking was his passion. He could take an existing recipe and add his own take on it to create a new culinary wonder. He won several awards in France and eventually won a full scholarship to Le Cordon Bleu Culinary Arts School in Paris.

Enwain had it easy and was so talented that he wrote his own ticket for life. The Haggler family had picked him up after he graduated from Le Cordon Bleu. He was 23.

That night he was preparing his Boeuf Bourguignon, Moules-frites, and Banana Tarte Tatin for dessert. He pulled out all the stops to help everyone in the house forget about their troubles. At least for one night. That was his power and that was why he was paid more than any restaurant in the world would pay him.

Every meal with Chef DeDaure was a pleasure trip for the taste buds.

Anderson had already left. He never wanted the chef to pack him a lunch. He said that if he couldn't eat with the family, he would have to wait until he could.

Sam had left a few hours earlier. He was invited to stay for dinner but enjoyed eating alone. He hated to see the different eating habits of people who shared the same table with him.

Of course, he didn't tell the Hagglers that. He just said he had plans.

Rachel and Griffin were seated at opposite ends of the dining room table as Alexandra set the table. The amazing smells coming from the kitchen almost made Rachel forget about her traumatic experiences. Bentley wasn't feeling well. Even after Griffin brought him some Pepto Bismol, his stomach was still acting up.

Griffin had noticed something about the Haggler house. Whenever anyone showed aggression of any kind, his dead sister would appear.

Before Griffin could make a comment about loving the chef's food for the hundredth time, the doorbell rang. Rachel raised her brow at Griffin, with an almost mental reminder that he was still part of the hired help.

Alexandra took off toward the front door when Griffin stopped her. "No, Alex. I'll get this one." He smiled as he walked to the door. He opened the door and just stared at the person on the other side.

"Hello, Jason," said Deirdre Hallsey, with a smile.

***

Griffin entered the dining room and took his seat. He looked nervous about something.

A few moments later, Deirdre came into the dining room as well. She had a huge fake smile for everyone there. "Hello Hagglers! And Jason! And Haggler's staff!"

Rachel glared at Jason and then got up from the table. She approached Deirdre and spoke in a whisper. "Why are you here?"

Deirdre did her best to keep her smile. "I'm so sorry for any inconvenience. I'm not barging in you know."

"You weren't invited to dinner, Deirdre," Rachel snapped back, in a louder voice. We haven't heard from you in weeks and now you just pop up at dinner time. Aren't you making enough money selling houses, sweetie?"

Deirdre lost her smile altogether. "Look, Mrs. Haggler. I came here, because I needed to tell you something about this house."

"No more bullshit about Katie Elkton!" Rachel screamed. The house went dead silent as Deirdre took a step back. Rachel composed herself as the wound on her right thigh throbbed when Katie's name was mentioned. She assumed it was just a muscle reflex of some kind.

"I can see when I'm not wanted," Deirdre said, as if she was trying to get sympathy.

"You weren't invited, you stupid bitch!" Rachel yelled.

"Okay, come on man!" Griffin added. "What the hell has gotten into you Rachel? I mean…Damn!"

Griffin realized at the last minute that he made a serious mistake after successfully getting Rachel's attention.

"You are nothing but a hired hand Jason! You have no right to speak to me, unless I pull your fucking string! Did I speak slowly enough for you?"

Both Chef DeDaure and Alexandra glared at Rachel. "What?" she exclaimed. She stuck her chin out to her staff as if to challenge them in some way.

Griffin couldn't believe how Rachel was behaving. He stood up. "Deirdre. Why don't you and I go get a burger or something?" He stared down Rachel. "The air just got really thick in this house."

Rachel had a wild look in her eyes. One that neither her staff nor Griffin recognized. "You're going nowhere Jason," Rachel huffed. "If you leave this house, then don't ever come back!"

Griffin looked at Alexandra and the chef who were still staring. He then looked at Rachel and finally at Deirdre who had a look of complete confusion as to why she was treated that way.

He then looked back at Rachel. "Okay. I quit. Oh and since I don't work for you anymore..." He leaned in close to her face. "...you're a bitch and a whore. I wouldn't take you if it came with a house and an expense account."

Rachel slapped him hard. Her eyes were crazier than they were before. He just placed a hand on his red cheek and smiled. He decided to see how far he could push her.

Deirdre ran into the bathroom. She locked the door and placed her hands on the sink while she stared into the mirror. "Please, please, please, please," was all she said as she closed her eyes.

***

Anderson came into the dining room looking pissed. "Damn it Rachel! I can hear you all the way outside! What the hell is your problem?"

Rachel grabbed her hair with both hands and let out a blood curdling scream. "Nooooo! I swear if someone asks me that one…more…time…"

Anderson looked at Griffin. Griffin threw his hands in the air. "Look dude! I didn't touch her!"

Rachel started to calm down when she saw Anderson. She almost appeared submissive. "It's…my fault. Deirdre Hallsey came in uninvited and it set me off."

"I'll say," Griffin added. "By the way, I quit. You can give me some severance pay or a car or something for my troubles."

"Quit?" Anderson queried. "Why did you quit? Weren't the living arrangements to your liking?"

"Oh yeah," Griffin replied. "Everything was just great. Everyone under this roof seems to have serious anger management issues and..." He couldn't finish his sentence, because he looked around the dining room and realized that something was missing. Every time, before when someone expressed anger, Katie would show up in some manifestation or another. He fully expected his dead sister would show up, especially after Rachel let loose with everything she had.

"If you want to leave, I can't stop you," Anderson said. He walked up to Alexandra and Chef DeDaure. "I apologize for any commotion this evening. You don't get paid to listen to this. If you could wait in the living room until I get this squared away, I would appreciate it. Everything smells great chef!"

The two staff members reluctantly and silently walked slowly toward the living room.

Anderson addressed the situation between Griffin and Rachel. "Rachel. I strongly recommend you take several therapy sessions with Dr. Constance. He seems more than competent to handle whatever problems you have."

Rachel looked up at him in anger.

"Jason," Anderson continued, as he ignored his wife's look. "Your work has been really good. If it wasn't for the personality conflict you have with my wife, your work would be exceptional."

Griffin shrugged his shoulders as Anderson continued, "I would like it if you would stay on, in spite of the conflict. Rachel is an acquired taste. Yes, she's beautiful, but she also is a little whirlwind, if you don't know how to handle her properly."

"Hey!" Interrupted Rachel. "I'm standing right here!"

Anderson ignored her again. "I'm tired. I've been working more on my supposed vacation than I ever did at work. I really don't want to deal with this madness anymore. Is there any way you two can get along?"

"Is that the only choice here?" Griffin asked.

"You could leave as you wanted to before, Jason," Anderson replied. His smile was comforting. "I do think that this working relationship can be salvaged."

"How do you know that?" Griffin queried.

Anderson laughed. "That's what I do for a living! Just give it a little while longer. If after say…two weeks, you can't work together, then you can leave and I'll give you an amazing severance package that includes a car!"

Griffin chuckled as Rachel remained quiet.

"Jason. I may not be able to control a lot of what goes on in my own house, but I will say… I promise you it *will* get better."

Just then the doorbell rang.

May 8, 2014   9:04pm

Alexandra left the living room to answer the door. She heard absolutely nothing coming from the kitchen and assumed Anderson

Haggler had once again saved the day. She smiled as the chef gave her two thumbs up. He chuckled to himself as he leaned against the doorway leading from the entry hall into the living room.

"I got it!" Alexandra called out. She had an almost singsongy tone in her voice. She breathed a sigh of relief as she approached the front door. She was looking forward to tasting Chef DeDaure's Banana Tarte Tatin. She had never eaten so many exotic foods since he showed up to work for the Hagglers.

Alexandra had vacation time coming up in the winter. She had planned on going back to Greece to see her niece, Gracie. She had seen Gracie grow up in the pictures that were emailed to her by her brother, but there was no replacing a real hug. Gracie was much older, but that wouldn't stop Alexandra from spoiling her rotten.

She carried the happy thoughts of Gracie and her brother with her as she opened the door with a smile.

The smile slowly disappeared and was replaced with a look of horror as the sound of one gunshot rang out through the dead silence of night.

A hole appeared in her forehead as blood started to trickle from it. She had time to shed one tear. Alexandra was dead before she hit the floor.

The assailant came in, closed and locked the door, uncaring and unmoved by what had just occurred.

It was as if everything that followed, happened in slow motion. Anderson, Rachel, and Griffin stopped talking in the dining room when they heard the gunshot. The only thing they shared was a look of shock. Anderson grabbed Rachel and ran toward the basement.

"I'm not going in there," she whispered.

"Do you want to live?" Anderson asked.

She followed him into the basement.

The chef tried to run back into the living room as he cried out. He overturned furniture in hopes that it would slow down the assassin.

Griffin rushed through the kitchen to the hallway. He had just made it to the entrance to the living room in time to see Chef Enwain DeDaure run for all he was worth toward him. He stopped short as two more gunshots echoed through the house. A small trail of blood flowed from the left corner of his mouth.

Griffin could feel the chef's eyes plead with him to somehow help him. He was beyond help as he dropped to his knees and then fell forward.

Griffin stepped behind the doorway to the kitchen by the refrigerator, as the assassin stepped over the chef's body and stopped at the doorway.

There was a 9mm Smith and Wesson handgun in the right hand of the assassin. There was a thin trail of smoke coming from the barrel.

Griffin jumped out from behind the doorway and grabbed the gun with both hands. Even *he* couldn't understand his bravery. He chalked it up to not wanting to die, which put him in a Catch-22.

He raised his arms as he moved the gun and the assassin's arms into the air to prevent anyone from getting shot. He really didn't have time to see who he wrestled with, but he did figure out two things. The assassin was strong and wore a police officer's uniform.

The struggle caused the two to bump into the wall in the hallway. Upon contact with the wall, their arms swung down with the gun about waist level. Griffin saw who he was fighting with, as the gun went off.

***

Sheriff Donovan had put in a long day as usual. Little did he know, it was about to get a little bit longer. He was in the kitchen of his home with his wife waiting for him in bed. He was hungry.

He always had a Turkey Bologna and Swiss cheese sandwich with Honey Mustard before he went to bed.

He was about to take a bite, when his cell phone rang. Sheriff Donovan carried that thing everywhere he went. He liked to be available.

Setting the sandwich down, he reluctantly answered the phone. "Donovan. This better be important, because you may have woken up my better half and for sure you're keeping me from a date with this sandwich."

"Sheriff," said the voice on the phone. It's Harper. Sorry for bothering you, but we got two calls of disturbing the peace. It appears someone has been firing off a gun inside a residence.

Sheriff Donovan rolled his eyes. "Damn it! How many times have I told Caleb to make sure his .22's unloaded before he goes to bed?" He looked around to make sure he didn't raise his voice and wake up his wife.

"It ain't Caleb this time," Harper replied. "That's why I called *you*. You said you wanted to handle any call personally if it was from or about 2782 Sedgewood Drive."

The sheriff's heart picked up a few extra beats. "The shots came *from* the Haggler house?"

"Yes sir, Sheriff. You want me to send someone?" Harper asked hesitantly.

"No," the sheriff replied. "I'll take care of it. If I need help I'll call it in."

"Roger that," Harper said as he hung up.

May 8, 2014   10:26pm

It took Sheriff Donovan 45 minutes to get dressed and tell his wife he had to go out, before he pulled up to the Haggler house. He parked his cruiser on the opposite side of the street.

The sheriff sat for a moment and took note of the cars that were parked in or near the driveway of the house in question. He saw Rachel's Escalade, but there was another vehicle there too. He recognized the blue Hyundai with a missing rear bumper. Deputy Alana Sachs.

"Oh Sachs. What are you doing here?" He said out loud, as if she could hear him. He got out of the car and crossed the street carefully. One of the neighbors who must have called in the gunshots peeked out of their kitchen window. The sheriff saw them and waved them back away from the window.

As he stepped onto the sidewalk in front of the Haggler house, he saw another car parked on the side. *Deirdre was inside as well.*

He let out a sigh and made his way to the front door. He couldn't put his finger on it, but there was something strange about the house. It had always been strange, but there was…*something else.*

He couldn't look in through any of the bottom floor windows, because there was some kind of red fabric or something else with a red hue that covered them from the inside. He got out his cell phone and attempted to call Deputy Sachs. There was nothing but static. The same thing happened when he tried to call Deirdre.

He unsnapped his holster and reached forward to press the doorbell. As soon as his hand came within a few inches of it, he felt an intense shock that knocked him back. He grabbed his hand in pain as he looked at the black scorching of his index finger. "What the hell?" He stepped back from the door and looked at the house in fear.

He never really believed all of those things about Katie Elkton that he heard from Deirdre. He assumed the same thing that mostly everyone else did. The ghost of Katie was created to bring in tourists. He didn't know how to deal with *this.*

"Perhaps, Sheriff Donovan, the answers do not lie within the house itself." The voice came from behind him. The sheriff turned around ready to draw his weapon, when he saw a tall thin man dressed in a suit. The man had a thin tie and wore glasses. "Please don't draw your firearm on me. I may have had displeased clients, but I have done nothing to deserve an early death. Allow me to introduce myself. I am Dr. Samuel Constance."

Sheriff Donovan looked at Sam suspiciously. "You're that shrink the mayor sent the Hagglers to for help."

"Bravo on getting that fact right," said Sam, as he pretended to clap. "Please don't ever call me a *shrink* again. It is completely inappropriate and rather offensive. Would you like me to call you bacon? No, I thought not."

"Why are you here *Doctor*?" Sheriff Donovan had started to lose his patience.

Sam smiled and looked up at the house. "I am here to stop you from making a serious mistake, my *law enforcement friend*."

The sheriff walked up to Sam. "Are you being friendly now, or just trying to make up for the *bacon* crack?"

"Obviously," Sam responded. "As for how I knew you'd be here, I simply monitor the police scanner I recently purchased. Since there's not a lot of crime going on in our fair burb, it was easy to figure out what the more interesting things were and where I needed to be. Of course, you also know I now have a vested interest in the occupants of this house."

"Maybe you can tell me what's going on with the electric doorbell and why the red windows then," the sheriff said accusingly.

Sam put his hands behind his back. "On the contrary, my dear Sheriff. I have neither the desire, nor the compulsion to investigate things that are not only of no interest to me, but outside the realm of my expertise. Always stay with what one knows, I always say."

Sheriff Donovan tried to hide his frustration. "So I'm going to ask you again then, Doc. Why…are…you…here? This isn't a spectator sport."

Sam chuckled. "It's not a *sport* at all, Sheriff. However, I have some questions as to the authenticity of certain instances involving the Haggler family, which I need to investigate further."

"Well, you're not going to find your answers in there…" answered the sheriff, "…unless you know a way to turn off the electricity. For some reason, there's a weird electrical field around the whole house and I can't find a way in without getting fried."

Sam sighed. "Perhaps I have not made myself clear. Such is the case from time to time. Even I have a hard time following what I'm saying. Haha! Anyway, I am not here for the Hagglers. I am here for you. The investigation that I am talking about, would greatly benefit from a law enforcement official being present."

"So you're saying that you need the law to get you into places that you might not be able to get into otherwise," Sheriff Donovan said, confidently.

"See Sheriff?" Sam responded. "We do speak the same language. I have two inquiries. Both of which need to be addressed immediately, or sooner if possible. This would of course, mean that you would have to relinquish your standing guard over the Haggler's lawn."

"I can't leave until I make sure everything's okay on the inside of the house. And anyway...how can I trust you?" The sheriff replied.

Sam walked closer to the sheriff. "My dear Sheriff. You don't have to trust me. Know that Mayor Sutton requested my assistance with the Haggler family. The mayor trusts me, you trust the mayor. Therefore, you must trust me by association. If there is absolutely nothing you can do until the bizarre electrical disturbance has passed, then perhaps you should call someone else to watch the house while you are away with me. I'm sure if anything else happens, they will inform you."

The sheriff shook his head trying to catch all of the doctor's mumbo jumbo. "I don't like leaving the scene of a disturbance, but alright. I have to call for back up, because there was a gun fired from inside the residence. You said we need to go now?"

"Yes," Sam answered. "Or sooner. I appreciate the fact that you feel the need to feed me information on how you plan to do your job, but I feel confident you will make the right call. If you need validation, I can say that I didn't vote for you, but I echo the sentiment of Lakeshore in putting their safety in your capable hands. If our investigation is as successful as I anticipate, then they could promote you to a higher status than sheriff, if such a position exists. Other than Mayor of course."

"Damn Doc!" Exclaimed Sheriff Donovan. "Don't you ever shut up?"

For the first time in his adult life, Sam felt embarrassed. He tried his best to recover. "Onward to Haggler Industries, Sheriff. I believe Albert Singer is in charge when Anderson Haggler is away. Time is ticking. Tick. Tock."

Twenty

May 9, 2014   1:18am

The Lakeshore police cruiser pulled up to the twenty story building. Sheriff Donovan and Dr. Samuel Constance exited the cruiser and headed toward the glass double doors in the front.

A man in his mid-40s stood on the inside of the doors. He didn't look pleased at all. He was about 6 feet tall and had a slight beer belly. He was bald, but it looked like it was his decision and not one made by nature. He had strong hands, which told Sam that he had probably worked hard manual labor when he was younger. He was dressed in a polo shirt and casual slacks.

Sheriff Donovan had called ahead to make sure someone would be there.

Albert Singer unlocked the doors and stood with obvious impatience. "I hope you know that I am unaccustomed to being woken up at this hour. With our CEO away, I have been doing more than my share."

"This is no picnic for us either, Mr. Singer," the sheriff huffed. "We've been on the road for a couple of hours and I am in no mood to be out here either. If we can just come inside..."

"No Sheriff," Singer replied. "My cooperation ends at the front door. Whatever you have to ask me, you can do so right here. You're a little out of your jurisdiction. Aren't you Sheriff?"

"This pertains to a matter in Lakeshore of which I cannot give you any information about," replied the disgruntled sheriff. "Is Anderson Haggler on some kind of leave and if he is, how long has been on it?"

Sam nodded with approval.

Singer sighed. "He's been gone about a month I suppose. He's not due back until about the middle of June."

The sheriff and Sam rehearsed their questions in the car, so that they would cover all of the bases needed. "To your knowledge, did Mr. Haggler return at any time for the purpose of work, or just to say hello?" The sheriff queried.

Singer adjusted his stance. "I've actually been monitoring the video feeds, just in case he *did* stop in. He hasn't been here. He left a strict message that he was not to be disturbed at his cabin. It was supposed to be a family outing. It must be going well, since he hasn't even checked in. That goes against everything I know about Anderson."

Sam looked confused as he remembered everything that Anderson said about going to work. He was absent from the Haggler house more than he was there.

Sheriff Donovan waited for the affirming nod from Sam. He got it. "Mr. Singer. One more question please. Where exactly is the location of Anderson Haggler's cabin?"

Twenty one

May 9, 2014   1:25am

Anderson, Rachel, and Deirdre sat on the sofa in the living room. Griffin had the 9mm pointed at the assassin.

Deputy Alana Sachs looked horrible. She was pale, shaky and extremely sweaty. She sat on the floor directly in front of Griffin with her hands tied in front of her with twine. There was one of Anderson's belts tied tightly around her right thigh, just above where she had been shot during the struggle with Griffin.

Deirdre was still shaking and breathing with her mouth open. Anderson glared at Deputy Sachs as Rachel was crying and kept playing with her hair while avoiding eye contact with the deputy.

"What kind of monster are you?" Griffin snapped. He knew he was in a position of power and wanted everyone to see him as a hero. "You killed two people in cold blood! What the hell?"

Deputy Sachs looked up at Griffin. She grimaced and almost doubled over from the pain in her stomach. It had seemed to intensify since she entered the house. "Poison...I was poisoned."

Rachel stood up in anger. "Poisoned? So go to a damn doctor! What do we have to do with your problems?"

Deputy Sachs slowly turned her head toward Rachel. "Lobster...Bisque...poisoned."

Rachel tried to attack the deputy, but Anderson held her back. "You lying bitch! My staff isn't responsible for your bullshit! You probably picked up an STD and now you're trying to pin it on us so you can bleed our bank account!"

Griffin looked at Rachel with surprise. "Whoa! You got way too much time on your hands to think up scenarios like that."

Deputy Sachs started to tremble and shake as Deirdre freaked out. "It's Katie Elkton, I tell you! Katie's doing it all!"

"Will someone please shut her up?" Griffin barked. "I can't think straight with all this noise!"

"Well then, maybe you're not the perfect choice to be holding a lethal weapon," Anderson replied calmly.

Griffin approached Anderson. "Oh, you'd like that! Mr. big shot Haggler is in charge of everything he sees!" He started to unknowingly wave the gun around during his tirade. "You have everything man! You have a hot wife, a great job you can go to whenever, and a bank account that anyone would kill for!"

The room got quiet as Griffin thought for a moment about the situation he was in. He had a gun to a wealthy man and woman. He looked at Deirdre and realized she was so hysterical, he could have made her say anything to back him up. He then looked at Deputy Sachs and saw his scapegoat. Griffin was one brief step away from getting enough money to set him up for life. He could go to a country without an extradition treaty with the states and live a life of luxury. Then he could get women like Rachel to bend to his will. He was one step away from fulfilling all of his dreams. All he had to do was get Anderson to give him a lot of money, kill him, Rachel, and Deirdre and blame it on Deputy Sachs.

The deputy had created that situation. All he had to do was go one…step…further.

The bad thing about Griffin's thoughts turning to darkness, was that everyone in the room knew where his mind was going. Just by his expression.

"Give me the gun, Jason," Anderson said, with his hand held out.

Bentley walked into the living room rubbing his eyes. "Mommy? I heard noises. I can't sleep. I think Katie's gone."

May 9, 2014   2:56am

"Well at least the cabin's closer to Lakeshore," Sheriff Donovan said, sarcastically.

Sam had been quiet for most of the trip to the Haggler's cabin. He was trying to prepare himself for any possibility. The most reasonable premise was finding Anderson and his pregnant ex-secretary at the cabin, which would explain his lie about having to work. Sam was sure it had to be work, having a wife and a mistress. The secretary must have something special to make Anderson break his old habits of going to work at every opportunity.

The sheriff's cruiser pulled up to a beautiful little cabin nestled in front of a group of tall Spruce Trees and about 100 feet away from a fresh water lake. There was a stump with an axe by it where firewood was chopped. There was a large Oak Tree next to the house. A large over hanging branch had a tire swing tied to it. The cabin itself appeared to be handmade using short-leaf pine logs. There was an old welcome mat with the words, "If you found this cabin, you must have followed us" on it.

There were two windows in the front of the cabin, with curtains drawn on both.

Sam and the sheriff stepped up to the front door. "I'm sure you already figured out what we're going to find in there, Doc," Sheriff Donovan said, with a smile.

Sam smirked, covering up his nervousness. "I appreciate the vote of confidence. Perhaps you confuse me with a television detective, who seemingly has more answers than he has resources for. I would like to think that my many years of paying attention to body language and not necessarily to *what* is said, but *how* it is said, would provide some assistance in this matter. I would also like to point out, there could be other factors that I am unaware of, which could change the outcome from anything I was prepared for. I am basing my intuition not on a preponderance of evidence, but the repetition at which Mr. Haggler insisted that he had to work, which was already proven to be a lie. The other piece of psychiatric detective work, would involve the fact that Mr. and Mrs. Haggler had a number of arguments concerning this particular cabin in question. What was odd was that Mrs. Haggler appeared to cut her husband off when he was about to go into details about the problems surrounding the events that transpired in this cabin. I suspect we will find something suspicious inside."

Sheriff Donovan rolled his eyes. "Damn! Don't you ever stop talking? I swear as long as I've been married, my wife has never talked as much as you just have!"

Sam cleared his throat. "Might I add, Sheriff, that had I not said anything, we would not be here at this moment about to unveil a deep dark secret in Anderson Haggler's life."

"Whatever," the sheriff added, as he tried the door.

It was unlocked.

The sheriff looked at Sam as if he had the answer. Sam looked apprehensive. The sheriff pushed the door open wide. The men were immediately hit with an overpowering and putrid smell. The sheriff had a slightly stronger stomach than the psychiatrist, but he had to hold his hand over his nose and mouth anyway.

Sam stepped away from the cabin and proceeded to empty his stomach of just about everything he had eaten the previous day.

Sheriff Donovan took out his gun and slowly walked into the cabin. He coughed every once in a while, because of the stench. He walked through the living room after realizing the smell came from deeper inside the cabin.

Sam composed himself and removed a handkerchief from one of his pockets. He placed it over his mouth and nose and followed after the sheriff.

He caught up to the lawman just outside of the master bedroom door. They both had fearful looks as the sheriff noticed several sets of scratches on the outside of the door. Almost as if several different animals tried to get inside the room. Sam stood behind the sheriff.

Sam realized at that point the situation probably wasn't anything like he had deduced.

The sheriff slowly pushed open the door as his heart raced. Once the door was open, they could both see the origin of the rancid smell.

The men were not prepared for what they saw lying on the floor of the master bedroom of the cabin. The look of horror on both of their faces was enough to know that they would never forget it as long as they lived.

***

Skye Hallsey was almost asleep. She usually couldn't get to sleep until early in the morning. Her mind was on the Hagglers and of course, Katie Elkton. She had done everything in her power to avoid the Haggler house. She thought she could then avoid the nightmares.

The last nightmare she had was several days before. Every time she closed her eyes, she could still see the grisly picture of Bentley

Haggler swinging from his mother's entrails. The descriptive dreams she had bothered her. She could make out every detail. She had never met Deputy Alana Sachs and wondered why she was the main focus of that particular dream.

She didn't bother to tell anyone about her dreams or her visions. She considered them to be one in the same. Her mother didn't even seem to care that Skye had returned home. They never talked, so it really wasn't that big of a surprise. Of course, knowing something and actually experiencing it are two different things. She had always hoped her expectations would be raised by something positive.

No such luck.

Skye felt that she was cursed. She didn't belong in Lakeshore. She didn't know anyone else quite like her. No one else she knew dressed like her or even came close to her I.Q. One always cancelled out the other. People would look at her black clothes, hair, and makeup and feel sorry for Deirdre for having such a rebellious child.

If people only gave her a chance.

It seemed like the only people who wanted to be friends with Skye were no longer breathing.

She had a weird bond with the Haggler house that she couldn't explain. Then again, it may not have been the house at all. There may be a connection with one or more of the occupants of the house. Katie for one. *Maybe.*

To Skye, Katie was more than just one persona. Every time she had an experience with the deceased girl, Skye felt that there was something more than just Katie. In fact, she felt *Katie* was more than just Katie.

That's why she had no one to talk to about it. She felt that there wasn't anyone who would or could understand. If she had gone to a psychiatrist and mentioned what she thought, she would probably be locked away in some asylum. They would have to throw away the key with Skye, because she would never be able to tell anything but the truth. Even if it was the truth as she saw it.

She may not have known who Katie Elkton was when she was alive, other than what her mother repeated in her tour, but she did know that the breathing challenged Katie was not the same person. Whoever the new undead girl was, she was more of an amalgam of more than one persona.

Skye knew Katie Elkton had died and was *not* coming back wanting to play, or anything else. *Something*...or a lot of *somethings* had manifested into something recognizable. It was as if whatever it was that existed in the house had chosen the one vessel which had been mentioned over and over again in those damned tours. *The ghost of Katie Elkton.*

Skye believed her mother gave the entity a template to create an interactive persona.

Skye wasn't a religious girl, but she remembered one thing a friend of hers said, "Satan comes in the purest of forms."

She didn't know if that was from the Bible or just something a priest said to her friend once. Either way, it was more believable to her that Katie was *Satan*, than to believe it was really Katie.

So much for sleep. Skye sat up in her bed and sighed. She went to the living room and turned on the television. The Conjuring was on. *No thanks.*

She could hear her phone ring from her bedroom where she left it. A chill ran down her spine, as she hesitated to see if the voicemail would pick up.

It didn't.

Her *friends* didn't like to use voicemail. They preferred to talk to the living without the aid of electronic messaging. *Bet they don't text either.*

Her phone kept ringing. She walked to her mother's room. Deirdre wasn't there. She looked around and noticed her mother was nowhere in the house. Skye would have smiled at the thought of being alone, if it wasn't for the fact that someone wanted to talk to her.

She walked slowly back to her room. She stared at the incessantly ringing phone. She took a deep breath and turned on as many lights as she could, then answered her phone. "Katie?" She asked quietly.

There were strange noises coming from the phone, as if several people were muttering in a low unintelligible language.

"Skyyeeee," was the response on the other end. It sounded as if the voices were fading in and out as they spoke. It also sounded like they were taking turns talking. "Weeeee hhhaaaavvvee yyuuooorrr mmmooottthhheeerrr…"

Skye thought for a minute before answering. "Good for you. Let her know that I think she's a bitch."

"Biiitttccchhhh…" was their response. It was almost as if they mocked Skye. "Woooonnn'ttt sssttooppp wwwiiittthhh… hhheeeeerrrr. Nnnneeeeevvveeerrrr ssssstttoooppp…"

Skye hung her head down. "Shit. Looks like you better set another plate for dinner. I'm coming over."

Twenty two

May 9, 2014   3:32am

Skye arrived at 2782 Sedgewood Drive for what she believed to be her final visit. She was dressed in black jeans and a black turtleneck with the arms torn off.   She had on black fingernail polish, lipstick, and mascara.   She wore her black gloves with the fingers cut out as well. She figured she would dress for the party.

She knew the entity or *evil* wouldn't stop chasing her. It needed her because of their bond and because she could feel it for what it was. It was possible it had to eliminate everyone who knew what was going on.

She saw a sheriff's department cruiser parked in the street along with three vehicles in the driveway.

Deputy Andy Harper got out of his car when he saw Skye. "I'm sorry ma'am, but no one is allowed in the house until I get orders from the sheriff that it's okay."

Skye gave him a disgusted look. "I'm not a *ma'am* deputy. I'm 15 and a half. Maybe you can't get in, but it called me."

"What called you?" He asked,

"The house," she responded, almost not believing what she had just said herself. "Do you want to see the text?"

"It texted you?" He asked, completely oblivious.

Skye pointed to her mother's car. "Do you see that car? That's my mom's car. She needs me. Can I go in now?"

***

Deirdre was huddled in one corner of the sofa. She kept mumbling, "Katie's going to get us all."

Griffin had calmed down and was sitting on a chair. He left the gun on the coffee table after he decided there were more important things to worry about, than to hold the Hagglers hostage.

Anderson glared at Deputy Sachs. Her health was deteriorating. She dry heaved every few minutes and her face was almost completely white. She coughed up blood every once in a while.

Her trembling was more apparent. Griffin would watch her and then turn away with disgust. "What are going to do with the murderer?"

"She must have cut the phone and internet lines," Anderson answered.

"Did she seal the fucking house so we couldn't get out too?" Griffin asked with frustration in his voice.

"Just kill me," the deputy said. "If I get the chance, I'll kill...you all."

Griffin stood up and punched the wall. "Damn it! She needs to die!"

Anderson stood up as well. "Who's going to kill her, Jason? You? Do *you* have what it takes to take a human life?"

Rachel glared at her husband, while Bentley watched the television with headphones on.

Blood trickled down from Deputy Sachs' mouth as she started to cry. "Kill me damn you! Kill me now!"

"Fucking shut her up!" Yelled Griffin. His patience was gone.

"Stop cursing! Bentley might hear you!" Rachel yelled.

"We all just need to calm down," Anderson added.

"No!" Screamed Griffin, as he dove for the gun.

Rachel reacted the quickest as she dove for it too. They slammed into each other and slid over the table and onto the floor. Rachel came up with the gun. Anderson and Rachel's eyes met as she froze.

She remembered.

"Oh my...no," she said as she fell to her knees and started to cry.

"Finally," Anderson said, as if he knew something that everyone else didn't.

"Kill me!" Screamed Deputy Sachs again. "Can't...take the...pain."

"Alright, that's it!" Griffin declared, as he went over to the deputy. "This ends now!"

Griffin raised his closed fist as Deputy Sachs closed her eyes.

Deirdre screamed, "No! That's what Katie wants!"

As Griffin's fist rushed toward the deputy with all the strength he could muster, the front door blew open to reveal Skye just outside the threshold of the home. A warm wind blew toward Skye as she entered the house. The door slammed shut behind her.

She could feel everything unnatural that was inside of the house. It hovered and whispered around her as she dropped to her knees. "I never...dreamed...it was this bad." Her insides felt like they were being ripped apart and torn from her body.

Griffin's fist connected with the deputy's face with all of his hate and fury adding to the punch. Deputy Sachs fell over due to the force of his blow.

Bentley stood up and took off his headphones.

Deirdre had a look of pure horror on her face. "That's the catalyst to bring the real Katie out! Oh, please no! The one thing that should have never have happened in this house, has now happened."

"What?" Griffin asked. He was unsure if he should have hit the deputy, but it felt...*really good.*

Deirdre had a look of despair. "A man struck a woman."

Skye managed to arrive just in time. "She's right. We're not getting out of here now."

Deputy Sachs started to tremble and shake uncontrollably. The twine that was tied around her wrists burned off from some unseen force, leaving only charred marks on her flesh. She went into violent convulsions as she screamed for help.

No one could help her.

She convulsed until she ended up on all fours. She then started to dry heave again. The noises that were emitted from her throat were no longer human as tears streamed down her face. Her hands bled as they dug into the carpet in the living room. She pulled up pieces of carpet along with pieces of her skin.

Her screams slowly turned to an inhuman growl as blood started to spray out of her mouth with each cough. Everyone backed up to either one of the two exits from the living room, as the lights all over the house started to flicker.

Deputy Sachs' back arched like an animal that had been cornered. Something was moving violently in her stomach as she would vomit up blood in small quantities.

Something pushed from within her stomach as she hacked and wheezed out more blood. Her entire body was convulsing so much that she started to push any furniture near her, away with just a touch. Her mouth started to stretch as her head lowered.

The tortured screams resonated through everyone who watched. As grisly as it was, no one could turn away from the sight.

The skin on her mouth started to tear away as her mouth stretched out further. The cracking sound of the jawbone being wrenched away from the deputy's face made Deirdre pass out.

With Deputy Sachs' bloody jaw lying on the floor, she continued to convulse and vomit out more blood. There were small chunks of what looked like entrails in the vomit.

The lights flickered more with each heave. It was almost strobe-like, as larger pieces of the deputy's internal organs were being vomited onto the living room rug. Deputy Sachs collapsed but continued to vomit blood and organs. The blood had completely covered the floor in the living room.

The lights continued to strobe, which made it appear like everyone was watching the event through a mutoscope machine.

In spite of the fact that Deputy Sachs was no longer alive, there were still gurgling noises heard from her body.

All of a sudden the strobe effect stopped and all the lights went out. No one moved or spoke.

A low red light appeared in the living room. The twisted remains of Deputy Sachs were crumpled in a pile near the pool of blood, as well as the internal organs that were regurgitated from the body.

Deirdre started to wake up just in time to see the pool start to move. As if controlled by an unseen force, the solid pieces in the blood started to move toward each other. They began to push together, which made the pile grow.

As the pile grew larger, it started to take a specific shape. The larger pieces of organs and entrails joined together as if they were creating a living puzzle. *Living* being the optional word.

The pile stopped growing upward at about 4 feet and started to grow outward in two directions. Tentacle-like appendages pushed out from the bloody mass. The sloshing of bodily fluids moving and sculpting was enough to make everyone sick.

Griffin's mouth dropped in astonishment when he saw the appendages shaping into what appeared to be *human arms*. "It's forming…a person," he gasped.

It was obvious the one thing that the group needed to try to find, was a way out of the madhouse. Rachel picked up Bentley and ran with him to the stairs. Skye tried to grab her mother's arm, but Deirdre pulled away and went running back to the first floor bathroom. Skye looked at Anderson with recognition. She could see something in him that the others obviously missed. He showed no emotion as he stayed right where he was. Skye looked at Griffin. He nodded as they ran off toward the kitchen.

May 9, 2014   3:57am

Deputy Harper waited patiently for word from Sheriff Donovan about what to do next. He didn't want to bust into the house, because he thought he would need probable cause, but he wasn't sure he had it. Even with the fact that Skye Hallsey had disappeared inside the house about a half an hour ago.

It was better not to make a move without the sheriff's orders, even under the circumstances.

Almost as if on cue, he heard the familiar sound of static on his radio. "Harper. Are you there?" It was the sheriff.

Harper happily answered. "Roger that, Sheriff Donovan. I am still keeping an eye on the Haggler house."

"Good," said the sheriff on the other end of the radio. "Make sure no one goes in or out. We've got some disturbing news."

Harper stopped breathing. *Make sure no one goes in or out?* "Uh…Sheriff? What if someone already went in?"

There was silence as Harper could almost see the sheriff shaking his head with disappointment.

"Who was it Harper?" Inquired the sheriff.

"It was Skye Hallsey," replied the apprehensive deputy. "Actually, it was kind of weird. The door opened right up for her when she approached. She didn't even have to knock or anything."

There was a brief silence again.

The sheriff sighed over the radio. "Did anyone come out that you know of?"

Harper bit his lower lip. "No sir. No one."

"Good," replied the sheriff with a more positive tone. "We found two bodies in the Hagglers cabin. The Medical Examiner didn't take long to figure out that the two people found, had been dead for about a month or so. We are waiting on a positive I.D. now."

"I'm sorry, Sheriff," Harper said. "I guess it wasn't natural causes."

"No. It wasn't natural causes. They were both murdered. And Harper?" The sheriff continued, "One of them was a child. We have to wait for confirmation of the identities, but we're pretty sure we know who they are. I hope we're wrong. I pray we're wrong."

**

Skye and Griffin went into the kitchen. The red light was in there as well. "Screw this!" Griffin exclaimed as he pulled out a three inch long flashlight from his pocket. He pushed the button on the bottom and a strong beam of white light appeared.

Skye was impressed. "Wow! Nice job, but how is that supposed to stop us from getting ripped to shreds by an undead army?"

"Army?" Griffin asked. His face turned pale. "I thought it was just Katie."

She grabbed the flashlight and headed down the stairs to the basement. She stopped on the third step down and turned to face Griffin. "This has nothing to do with Katie Elkton. That's what *they* want you to think."

***

Deirdre closed and locked the first floor bathroom door behind her. The faint red light kept her in a constant state of panic. She trembled as she looked around for some sense of comfort. "Please don't kill me, Katie. I told people about you. I let them know what a tortured soul you are and that you need love and kindness."

She stepped into the bathtub and closed the plastic shower curtain in hopes that Katie wouldn't be able to find her, even if she came into the bathroom. She sat down and pulled herself into a fetal position.

Deirdre had almost convinced herself that Katie had no interest in her, when in spite of the door being locked, it opened slowly. She could hear a small creak. She started to cry and pray as she heard the sound of small barefoot feet on the wooden floor.

She heard something else as well.

Deirdre heard something similar to the sound of thin tree branches cracking and breaking. She tried to hold her breath, but she was breathing erratically to begin with, so that was out of the question.

Deirdre turned her head slowly toward the sounds. The red light was up to the shower curtain, but it was dark in the bathtub.

She could see a shadow form against the curtain. The shadow was of no one bigger than about 4 feet tall. Even in the shadow, the hair was noticeably matted and wild. The shadow's head slowly tilted to one side, while more cracking and breaking noises were heard.

Deirdre panicked and breathed rapidly through her mouth. "I didn't hurt you, Katie!" She yelled. "I tried to tell them that they needed to protect you!" She started to mentally lose it as she laughed after just about everything she said. "Haha! Katie! You and I are friends! I love you dear! I love you more than my own daughter! She's here somewhere! Haha! Maybe you can find her and play with her! She likes to play!"

Deirdre lowered her head as she repeated, "Please don't kill me."

The shower curtain was pulled back quickly to reveal the remnants of what used to be a little girl. Her hair was wet with blood. Her body was twisted and broken. Her hands were twisted with each finger broken in several places. Some of the fingers were broken off. Her neck was swollen with part of her spinal column protruding from the front of her neck. Her eyes were red and appeared to shimmer like water. Her lower jaw was almost detached as blood and puss routinely dripped from one side or the other. She wore a red dress stained in blood and mucous. Her legs were broken at the knees and twisted inward when she walked. Almost pigeon-toed. She wore no shoes and her left foot was twisted so that it almost faced the opposite direction.

Deirdre tried to scream, but no sound came out. She lost all hope when Katie tried to smile. "Kaaaattttiiiiieeee'sss nnnnooottt hheeerrreee," it slurred and groaned. It sounded like four or five people were trying to speak at the same time. "Yyyooouuu cccrrreeeeaaattteeeddd uuusss."

250

Deirdre finally managed to give voice to her scream.

***

Skye and Griffin had closed the basement door behind them. The red light was washed out by the abnormally powerful flashlight. Skye shined the light around to make sure there weren't going to be any surprises. She felt the soft earth beneath her as she walked. She looked down and started to feel uneasy.

Griffin noticed Skye's uneasiness. "What's up? Do you see Katie?"

"No," she said, almost unsure of why she was uneasy. "I don't know why, but I felt compelled to come down here."

Griffin started to feel uncomfortable. "What do you mean, *compelled?*"

Skye glared at him. "That's right. You don't know."

"Don't know what?" He asked. His voice was shaky. "You're not part of this Katie thing too are you? You're not going to deliver me to her. Are you?"

Skye would have been angry at his response if it wasn't for the constant uneasy feeling. "No! Don't you think that if I was going to kill you or deliver you to Katie, I would have done it before striking up a conversation?"

He nodded.

She continued. "There's something about this basement. I can't put my finger on it."

"Haven't been in the basement before?" He asked.

"I haven't been in this house before," she replied, while she kicked some of the dirt around. "The house has been trying to get me here for a while now."

Griffin was completely confused. "The house? What are you talking about?"

"You're not real smart for someone who is probably double my age," she replied with a little bit of condescension. "I *feel* things. It's kind of funny, because my mother always thought that *she* could. All she had was a feeling for where the money was."

Skye focused on kicking dirt around in one particular area. It was about five or six feet away from the bottom of the stairs.

Griffin became noticeably nervous. "What things do you feel?"

Skye looked at him accusingly. "What did you do? Oh hell! You did something. Didn't you?"

"Keep your voice down," he whispered.

"Oh please. If anything's going to find us, it's not because I raised my voice," she huffed. "I can feel something right here." She pointed the flashlight down on the ground.

"I'm sure it's nothing," Griffin said. She knew he *was* hiding something.

She threw him the flashlight and bent down. She picked up a garden trowel from a nearby shelf and proceeded to dig. She couldn't see his expression, because he had the flashlight practically in her face, but she knew he was nervous.

"Maybe we should concentrate on the issue at hand," he said, nervously.

"Tell me what it is that you don't want me to find out, if you want me to stop," she said, as she continued to dig. "I'll bet that whatever you're hiding has something to do with Katie."

Skye dug down about three feet, then she felt the trowel hit something. She shielded her eyes from the light as she looked up at Griffin. She then reached down and pulled out a human arm. She screamed and backed away as quick as she could.

Griffin came up to her slowly. "I'm not going to hurt you. There's no need for anyone else to get hurt."

"Who is this?" She asked, with fear in her voice.

He crouched down by her and took the light out of her eyes. "Let me start off by saying that my name is Griffin Elkton."

Skye's eyes widened with surprise. "Holy shit! You're Katie's brother!"

He nodded.

Griffin took a deep breath. "I guess it doesn't matter now. We're all probably going to end up dead anyway. My dad was abusive. My mother never stood up to him and I hated her for that. I hated him for hitting Katie and me. In 1994, my parents were in the basement and Katie was running toward them. She tripped on an upturned corner of a piece of tile and fell down the basement stairs to her death. Even though my parents weren't directly responsible for her death, I blamed them. After I saw her broken, lifeless body at the bottom of the stairs, I couldn't control myself. I ran down the stairs and grabbed the nearest thing I could that was heavy. I didn't care what it was. I just wanted to hurt them the way they hurt us. I grabbed a pick axe."

Skye grimaced.

Griffin continued as he started to cry, while he looked at the stairs. "I just kept hitting my dad while my mom watched in terror. There was blood everywhere. After I was done with him, I started on her. I don't know why. Maybe because I could. Anyway, when I finished, I buried them right here. I was okay with them being there, until the Hagglers moved in. I knew I had to make sure no one became suspicious about why I left the basement floor the way Jacob Reilly originally built it. Rachel Haggler wanted to cover the floor with wood or something. I couldn't take the chance that my parents would be sealed forever in the basement, just in case I might have had to move them or something. I didn't want their murders to be traced back to me."

Skye covered up the hole. "No reason to bring it up now. We have enough trouble. It explains some things though."

"I noticed something about Katie," he added, almost as an afterthought. "It seemed like every time someone got mad in the house, Katie appeared! Is that important?"

"Extremely," Skye replied. "I've been getting all kinds of weird feelings since I walked in this crazy house. I have a feeling that we'll get some answers from Rachel Haggler."

"What about Anderson?" He asked, with a questioned look. "He might know something."

She looked at him. "No. He won't be of any help. Did you see where Rachel and Bentley ran off to?"

Griffin thought for a moment. "Knowing Rachel, she took him up to his room. You do realize there's something out there trying to kills us, don't you?"

Skye grabbed the flashlight again and started up the stairs. "If something wants me dead, I want to know why. Take me to Bentley's room."

"How'd you get so smart for a kid?" He asked as he followed her up.

She laughed as they both reached the top stairs.

As they stepped onto the kitchen floor, they both heard a sound coming from the basement. It was a snapping and cracking sound. Skye stopped laughing as she and Griffin slowly turned and looked down into the basement.

Out of the darkness, a figure limped forward slowly toward the bottom of the stairs. It appeared to be a young girl covered in blood, with a body which was twisted and broken. They could see a bone sticking through the front of her neck. Her wheezing was loud and constant.

***

Bentley was sitting on his bed. The red light made it possible to see.

Rachel was on her knees holding his hands. "You know you're my precious angel. Don't you know that, Bentley?"

He sat still for a moment, then said, "Mommy? Why does my tummy hurt?"

Rachel started to cry. Her eyes were red and puffy from crying. "Well, honey. It's because you're upset that Mommy and Daddy always fight."

Bentley glared at her. "Why does my tummy hurt?"

Rachel questioned his pressure for an answer. "I told you sweetheart. I know it's not…"

She stopped talking, because the wound on her leg started to bleed through her pants. The pain was agonizing. "Baby. I'm being honest with you."

Bentley jumped off the bed and ran to the closet. He smiled as he pointed to a spot in the closet. "No! You lie Mommy! She's the only one who tells me the truth!"

Rachel got a cold chill as she couldn't see what he pointed at. "I always tell you the truth…"

The blood ran from her wound as if it were fresh. Her pants were soaked. "Damn it! What do you want me to tell you? What do you want to hear Bentley?"

Rachel had her back to the bedroom door. It opened as Griffin and Skye entered, then slowly closed. They remained quiet as they watched.

"What do you want from me?" She screamed.

Bentley tilted his head sideways. His voice had more bass in it. There was also almost a growl. "I want the truth, bitch. Can you handle that?"

Blood started to pour out from holes in his stomach and chest. Rachel ran to him and embraced him. As soon as she did, the room started to change right in front of Griffin and Skye. She looked around in awe and fear as the boy's bedroom slowly morphed. The walls changed into the wooden ones. The floor slowly changed into a sanded wooden one. The furniture also changed into a handmade bed with a quilt on it, a rocking chair, and another chair, plus a few end tables.

In no time at all, Bentley's room had transformed into an adult's bedroom in what appeared to be a cabin. Skye breathed in and could smell the fresh lake water that she knew was just outside. Griffin was almost in shock. He kept blinking his eyes as if that would wake him from whatever dream he thought he was having.

Rachel had Bentley locked in an embrace. She had her head pressed against his chest and her eyes closed.

Griffin opened his mouth to say something when Skye put her hand on his mouth and shook her head.

They watched the scene play out as if they were watching a television show, from inside the television.

Griffin and Skye's eyes widened as Anderson, Rachel, and Bentley walked into the bedroom. Anderson was happy. Rachel pretended to be.

"Bentley," Rachel said. "Why don't you go put your bags in your room? We're going to be here for a while."

"Okay, Mommy!" Bentley ran out of the room, but he had to stop because he started to cough.

"Be careful baby!" Rachel reminded.

Once her son was gone, she took a more serious tone. "Anderson. I know we came here to get some deserved family time, but we need to talk about something before we start having fun."

Anderson lost his smile. "What is it this time, Rach? We discussed that me cheating has put me on notice. Can we just get passed this? At least for Bentley's sake?"

"Oh you'd like to use your son to get out of this argument," She rebutted. "Maybe you'd like to talk about your *other* child too, while we're at it."

Anderson ran his hands over his face in frustration. "How the hell did you find out about that?"

"That's what you have to say to me?" She asked, while starting to cry. "That's your answer? How did I find out? Your bitch flapped her jowls when I paid her off. Hah! I bet you wondered why she quit soon after I caught you and her in your office. She can be bought! Who knew?"

"You had no right…" Anderson uttered.

"No right?" Rachel huffed. "I have every right to protect my child's inheritance! I have every right to protect my marriage!"

Anderson was enraged. "How is paying off the mother of my child…" He stopped himself before he could finish his sentence.

"I'm the mother of your child!" She returned with a fury of her own. "Not that whore who happened to be the flavor of the week!"

She sat on the bed and cried. After a few moments, her tears turned to uncontrollable laughter.

Anderson backed away from her. "What the hell is wrong with you?"

She kept laughing. "Haha! The funny thing is, after I paid her off, I kept wondering. What if she came back in our lives? What if that bastard were to grow up thinking that he or she had claim to Daddy's fortune? What if the little mongrel tried to take the bread from Bentley's mouth?"

Anderson panicked. "What did you do Rachel?"

"Simple really," she said nonchalantly. "After I paid the whore off, I hunted her down before she left the country. You should have seen her, Anderson. She was all packed up and ready to take the monstrosity growing within her to another place to start fresh."

Anderson gritted his teeth. "What did you do?"

Rachel smiled weakly. "I met her to wish her good luck and I even gave her a big hug to let her know that everything was alright. But you know what, Anderson? Everything wasn't alright. I took one of your hunting knives and used it to slice a nice little smiley face across her throat."

Anderson was torn between believing that she made up some sick joke and that she may have actually done what she said she did. "What? You sick fuck!"

"No darling," Rachel said as she moved to the end table and opened it up. "I could be considered sick, because of what I did next. I carved her stomach up like we do on Halloween with the Jack-O-Lanterns. I made sure there would be no way that *anything* inside of her lived.

Anderson slapped Rachel hard enough to knock her down.

She was still in front of the end table. "Go ahead and hit me!" She screamed. "Make me feel the pain for thinking about my son! There is nothing more important on this planet than Bentley! Not you! Not me! And certainly not some slut carrying your bastard child!" Rachel grabbed a handgun from the drawer. "Here's how it's going to play out, fucker! I'm going to kill you and then shoot myself. Bentley will then be sole heir to your fortune! No one can fight it! No one can deny who the real heir is! No one!"

Anderson was in shock as he backed away from her. He was at the doorway to the room when Bentley came in crying. "Mommy. What did you do? What did you do to that lady?"

Rachel panicked when she saw her son had heard every word she said. "No baby," she said, trying to make it better. "She was going to come between your daddy and me. She was going to try to take all of your money. I had to make sure that you got what's coming to you."

"Are you going to do to me, what you did to that lady?" Bentley asked.

Confusion swept over her. *He just didn't get it.*

"No, Bentley," she said. "I would never do anything to hurt you." She turned to Anderson with anger as she pointed the gun at him. "But Daddy is another story."

"No!" yelled Bentley. He jumped in front of his father as the gun went off.

Twice.

Tears rolled down Skye's face as Griffin remained in a state of shock.

"No!" screamed Rachel as she rushed to her child. Her child who she unloaded two rounds into. One ended up in his stomach, the other in his chest.

She picked up his head and embraced him while she howled in pain. She rocked back and forth which only succeeded in spreading Bentley's blood over a wider area on the floor.

She sobbed as Anderson was torn between calling the police and subduing his wife. He slowly approached her and could feel nothing but hate for the woman who just killed his son. He could feel his hands getting closer to her neck to snuff the life from her the way that she did with Bentley.

As he got closer, she turned toward him and pointed the gun in his face. "We're not finished yet!" She cried as she fired at his head.

Anderson did have a headache after all.

The room slowly morphed back into Bentley's room. Skye looked at Bentley with sympathy. She felt his pain.

Bentley pushed Rachel back away from him. "Mommy," he said in Bentley's real voice. "We're not finished yet."

Rachel smiled. "I know, baby." She embraced the boy she thought was her son for what appeared to be the last time. Anderson walked into the bedroom, despite it being locked and smiled as he joined his family. As they embraced, Bentley and Anderson started to convulse and then slowly disappeared.

Rachel smiled as she faced Griffin and Skye. Her stomach started to rise as if she was pregnant. Her stomach continued to get bigger as Rachel screamed for her dead son. She managed to let out one final scream as her body convulsed and then exploded from the inside out. Blood sprayed everywhere as the resulting force from the explosion knocked Skye and Griffin through the closed bedroom door and onto the landing.

Sheriff Donovan and Sam drove up to the Haggler place in time to see every window on the house explode from the outside. Harper, the sheriff, and Sam shielded themselves from the shower of bloody glass.

When the dust settled, the sheriff, who was still shaking from the explosion, looked at Sam. "I bet this is nothing like you expected, Doc."

"That would be a safe bet, Sheriff," Sam replied.

Epilogue

October 31, 2015   2:45pm

Skye celebrated her 17th birthday by giving the tour of the Elkton/Haggler house. There had never seen more tourists than that year. They didn't come for the winter sports. They came for the house at 2782 Sedgewood Drive. Mayor Sutton had declared a day that remembered those who died in *and* because of that house. There were also charities set up in those names. Lakeshore was on the map to stay.

The only sanitarium in Lakeshore was founded by Dr. Samuel Constance. It was built to house and provide care to those who suffered from severe mental illness and anyone else who needed psychiatric care. After the events of that night, Deirdre Hallsey was committed to the sanitarium.

Rachel Haggler was never charged with murder. They never did find all of the pieces of her. It took them months to scrape her body down from the ceiling in Bentley's room. What was left of her was melted up there.

Skye had her long golden hair styled with waves. She had on a business casual suit with slacks and a matching jacket. She lost the black clothes and makeup. She also sold the real estate agency. All of her time was taken up with her tours and the website, with the new name, "The Lakeshore Evil".

She was at the conclusion of that particular day's tour. There were some parts of the house that were blocked off from visitors, because they just couldn't be cleaned properly.

Sheriff Donovan, Mayor Sutton, and Deputy Harper took the tour for the first time.

Skye led a crowd of fifty people toward the front door where she stood with her arms crossed in front of her. "I want to thank you all for taking part of this tour."

"I have a question!" Said one woman from the back of the crowd.

Skye smiled. "Of course, if you would like to come to the front. Also, please speak louder so everyone can hear your question."

A woman in her mid-30s came to the front. She was dressed in blue jeans and a T-Shirt that read, "I love Seattle." "Hi. I was just wondering. You explained what happened. I want to know what caused it all."

"Great question," replied Skye. "This house was a receptacle for psychic energy. It started when Griffin Elkton killed his parents out of rage because of the death of his sister. Even though it was an accident, Griffin blamed his father for Katie's death. Add to that, the unbelievable psychic energy that Rachel had when she brought in intense guilt and anger, because she had killed her husband, child, and her husband's pregnant mistress. Then you have to add Deputy Alana Sachs killing two staff members here. It was all caused by anger. Anger was the catalyst, if you will, that fueled the psychic fire. It all adds up to an amount of psychic energy so immense that it created what I call, Solid Energy Apparitions. The energy actually created solid apparitions that could talk, eat, and do everything a human could, except leave the house. They were bound by the house, because that's where Rachel brought them, unbeknownst to even her. She had convinced herself that her family was still alive and thanks to the apparitions…they were. I can assure you that there are no apparitions, spirits or otherwise trapped in the confines of this house anymore. Our cleaners work really well. I hope that answered your question."

The woman nodded.

"If there will be no other questions, I would like to thank everyone. This ends the tour."

People stopped by and thanked Skye. The woman who asked the question came up to her with the sheriff, Mayor, and Deputy Harper.

The deputy shook her hand. "Wow, Skye. That was amazing. I'd like to introduce my cousin to you. The woman with the great question. Skye Hallsey, meet KC Harper."

KC shook her hand. "Pleased to meet you KC."

KC smiled. "Actually, I have to tell you. My being here has only a small portion to do with the tour. Which was more than interesting by the way. I live in Seattle and I heard about Lakeshore all the way out there. I have been given permission by the mayor to ask you if you would assist me in writing a novel about what happened to the Elktons and the Hagglers."

Skye got excited. "How wonderful! I would be honored to help out! I'm sure all of the residents of Lakeshore would love to be a part of your book!"

"Great! It's settled then!" KC said as she clapped her hands together.

"Just one question KC," Skye added. "Is this your first book?"

"Yes, it is," she replied. "But be assured, I am no novice."

"Of course," she said, as she smiled. "I can feel things and I think you would be perfect to tell our tale. After all, this is more than just a tale of horror...

October 31, 2015 4:15pm

Everyone had left the house except for Skye. She sighed as she walked out the front door to go to her car. She was about to lock the door when she saw Griffin tending to the front lawn. He had a blank stare as she came out. "Hello Skye. Everything went well I take it?"

She smiled at him. "As always, *Jason.* As always. I am so glad that we were able to get you for the exclusive care of this special house. I don't know which one will give out first, you or the house! Haha!"

"It's not like I have a choice," he said, with frustration.

"We all have choices, Griffin" she said, as she glared at him. "Some of us just know when to make them."

Skye Hallsey locked up the house for the day. She was going to enjoy her 17th birthday.

As she walked down the sidewalk to her car, she sang a song that helped to make her who she was…

"Griff and Katie went in the closet,

to hide from a big baddy.

Mommy got hurt and so did Griff,

By a monster insider of Daddy."

Take a sneak peek into Lakeshore Sanitarium

Book 2

Prologue

December 19th, 2015

Christmas in Lakeshore was like a story book fairy tale. The streets were lined with tiny white lights and wreaths that hung from every light post on Main Street. The windows were decorated and shop owners went all out with decorating their storefronts. Even the hospitals made sure to deck the halls and brighten it up for the sick patients, especially the children. The only place in Lakeshore that did not partake in the Christmas spirit was the Sanitarium.

The founder of the Sanitarium, Dr. Samuel Constance always said that maintaining a sterile environment look all year round was the best way to treat those suffering from a mental illness. The walls were always white and the tile polished every night, leaving it shinny with no trace of dirt. Dr. Constance took pride in his

Sanitarium, especially with it being the only Sanitarium in Lakeshore.

The Sanitarium was home to many Lakeshore residents and also those residents in other states suffering from severe mental illness. Dr. Constance specialized in treating those who suffered from schizoaffective disorders. These patients could no longer tell the difference between what was real and what was not, and Dr. Constance worked with them on finding their way back to reality.

Some never found their way back to reality and lived in the confines of the Sanitarium until they died.

That morning when Dr. Constance pulled into his parking spot at the Sanitarium, he sat in his car staring up to the third floor windows of the adult floor for those who suffered from a less severe mental illness. The white curtains all closed, hung lifeless, giving the impression that no one was inside.

That wasn't the case. The third floor held over 20 adult patients who suffered from depression, anxiety and other disorders that did not require constant supervision.

As Dr. Constance stared at the windows, his thoughts went back to a night he would never forget.

A night that would change him and his Sanitarium forever...

May 9th, 2014 was the night that Dr. Constance and Sheriff Donovan discovered two bodies in a cabin just outside of Lakeshore. Bodies that belonged to what he believed to be two living beings: Anderson Haggler and Bentley Haggler. The horror and mayhem that followed happened that night at the Haggler house in Lakeshore was something out of a horror movie. Dr. Constance never imagined such evil could exist, nor did he think he would ever come in direct contact with the evil that was in that house. The only two survivors of the events that took place at the Haggler house were Deirdre Hallsey and her daughter Skye.

Crippled by the fear she witnessed that night, Deirdre was now a patient in the Lakeshore Sanitarium. The evil she claims to have seen left her without the ability to speak. When the police arrived that night at the Haggler house, Deirdre was found hiding in a bathtub rocking back and forth whispering a name that Lakeshore residents will forever remember...

Katie Elkton…

Seven months later and several intense therapy sessions with Dr. Constance, Deirdre was still not speaking. A woman who took such pride in her appearance now looked battered and 30 pounds thinner. After five months of unsuccessful therapy treatments Dr. Constance moved Deirdre to the 5th floor of the Sanitarium. The 5th floor housed Lakeshores severely mentally insane. The patients on this floor were under constant nurse supervision in case someone got the idea to harm themselves or others. It was also the only floor in the Sanitarium that once a patient was moved to they never left…. Alive.

A nurse leaving her shift waved pulling Dr. Constance out of his thoughts. Shaking his head, he waved as the nurse walked passed his car.

Pushing the memories back from the night of May 9th, 2014, Dr. Constance stepped out of his car and adjusted his jacket. He ignored the uneasy feeling he had in the pit of his stomach and grabbed his leather briefcase and made his way into the Sanitarium. Before he even reached the front doors his cell phone beeped, notifying him that he had an urgent matter to attend to.

The message read Dr. Constance you are needed immediately on the 5th floor in room 2C. Code Grey.

The uneasy feeling that he tried to ignore returned, with full force. He didn't need the patients chart to know who was in room 2C. He knew very well who the person was in that room and knew it was only a matter of time before a situation escalated to the matter it had.

He stood in front of the locked door to room 2C and looked into the viewing window that was in the door. A dim light lit the room, giving Dr. Constance enough visibility to scan the room before entering. The patient sat on their knees on the bed with their back facing the door, restrained in a straitjacket.

Dr. Constance signaled for the nurse at the desk to unlock the door as two Orderlies came to assist him.

"What is the problem today with Miss. Hallsey?" asked Dr. Constance as they entered the room.

"She woke up screaming. She was uncontrollable and combative. We tried everything to calm her down before we administered a sedative and placed her in the restraint jacket," said the nurse on his left.

"I see." Dr. Constance stood beside the bed and observed before he tried to speak with the patient. "She seems to be calm now. Let's wait another hour before you remove the restraints, Linda."

"Yes of course Doctor," Linda replied.

He removed his pen from his coat pocket and wrote down his observations of the patient in a chart and pulled out his pocket flashlight. The light coming from the pocket flashlight flickered.

"Dammit, I just changed these batteries last week." he shined the light in the patients left eye and then the right eye.

Her skin was pale and her hair a matted oily mess. The dark circles and bags under her eyes were a result from lack of wanting to sleep. Or rather fear of sleeping because of what she might dream.

"Everything seems to be in order here. I don't see any psychical signs of change or harm that she tried to cause herself." Dr. Constance turned towards the door only to be stopped by a humming sound that came from the patient. He turned on his heel and listened.

"She has been doing that all morning, Doctor," replied one of the nurses.

It was a faint humming of some sort of song, almost nursery rhyme like. The nurses watched as Dr. Constance observed the behavior. The humming got louder and more recognizable.

"Is she humming the Jack and Jill nursery rhyme?" asked Linda.

"It would appear to be some version of that song. I have a feeling based on my interaction with this woman before she was placed under my care that she was not the type of mother to sing nursery rhymes to her daughter. We can call this a very tiny small step in the direction toward the progress of Miss. Hallsey speaking again." Dr. Constance gave one last look at the surroundings in the room and nodded, leaving the patient in the care of the two nurses.

He reached the door and turned quickly, facing the bed again. "Deirdre, it's great that you are taking small steps towards progress. It would be a shame for you to miss out on seeing your daughter, Skye, flourish into a young woman. She is doing wonders with The Lakeshore Evil tours."

The humming stopped and the room fell silent. Deirdre turned her head towards the door, her hair falling into her face. Her eyes met Dr. Constance and for a split second, it was as if he was looking at another person. He pulled his glasses off and rubbed his eyes only to open them again and see Deirdre sitting in the same position as he found her when he entered the room and humming the nursery rhyme again.

Also by KC Harper

Lakeshore Sanitarium Book 2

Whispers Book 3

It's love

Sweet something

Visit KC Harper on social media

www.facebook.com/Thelakeshoreevil

Follow on Twitter

@AuthorKC_Harper

Visit the website

www.kcharper.com